Kepler-438b

W. D. Smart

Kepler-438b

Publishing History
BSC E-Publishing
www.billsmart.com/bsc/e-publishing

Kindle Edition 1 / March 2015
Kindle Edition 1.1 / May 2015
Kindle Edition 1.2 / August 2015
Kindle Edition 1.3 / November 2015
Kindle Edition 1.4 / October 2016
Kindle Edition 1.5 / April 2017
Kindle Edition 1.6 / July 2019
Kindle Edition 1.7 / April 2020
ASIN: B00UW7QSPC

Paperback Edition 1 / March 2015
Paperback Edition 1.1 / May 2015
Paperback Edition 1.2 / August 2015
Paperback Edition 1.3 / November 2015
Paperback Edition 1.4 / October 2016
Paperback Edition 1.5 / April 2017
Paperback Edition 1.6 / July 2019
Paperback Edition 1.7 / April 2020
ISBN-13: 978-1507688755
ISBN-10: 150768875X

All Rights Reserved.
Copyright @ 2015 W. D. Smart

No part of this book may be reproduced or transmitted in any form or by any means, electronic or mechanical, including photocopying, recording or any information storage and retrieval system, without permission in writing from the author.

W. D. Smart

Dedication
...for my family around the world.

Books by W. D. Smart

Cap'n Billy – 2014

Kepler-438b – 2015

Jihadi – 2015

The Gliese Project – 2019
Book 1 – Helios
Book 2 – Kronos
Book 3 – Aeolus
Book 4 – Demeter

The Gliese Project – 2020
Consolidated Single Book

Acknowledgments

Thanks to all my friends, colleagues, and readers for their support and encouragement. I especially want to acknowledge the assistance of my good friend Madelaine and fellow author Jack Lourens.

Author's Note

Much of the technical information and figures used in this novel have been sourced online, especially from Wikipedia.com, but there is also a significant amount that is speculative, and some that are solely a product of my imagination – pure fantasy. For that reason, all the technical details, like the story itself, should be read and enjoyed entirely as fiction.

Contact Information

You may contact the author directly by email at:

WDSmart@BillSmart.com

Those wishing to leave comments on or engage in discussions about this book and its contents may do so on the *Kepler-438b* Facebook Page at:

www.Facebook.com/NovelKepler438b

Table of Contents

Table of Holograms and Figures

Kepler-438b

W. D. Smart

Chapter 1

Waking Up

*T*he jungle was a luscious feast for every sense. As he pushed his way through the underbrush, the towering canopy hovering above the jungle floor softened and filtered the light giving all the trees and plants an overall soft, green aura with small splashes of bright sunlight creating pools on the dark and mossy floor here and there. The air was cool and damp, just enough to be exhilarating without causing a chill. There was an earthy aroma of fallen trees, decaying plants, and rich loam. He could almost taste the fertile soil. He paused to allow the jungle to speak to him. Sighs came from the swaying trees, and the calls of birds echoed in the distance. Nearer, at his feet, soft clicks and scrapes were also testimony that the jungle was indeed alive.

Suddenly, a bright light pierced through the dark, green canopy accompanied by an irritating, raspy noise. He tried to turn away from the light, but it seemed to follow him. The raspy sound continued, staccato-like, and very annoying...

"GM-5! GM-5, can you hear me? Are you waking up?"

"What?" John responded with a barely audible grunt.

"What? Who?"

"GM-5! Wake up, laddie. It's time to rejoin the living," said the doctor with just the hint of a Scottish brogue as he activated the controls to rotate John's cryogenic pod from horizontal to a more upright position of about forty-five degrees.

Of course, terms for relative positions like "up" and "down" are really only valid in an environment subject to gravity. Here, on the spaceship, gravity was simulated by the centrifugal force generated by the rotation of the cylindrical hull of the craft around its core. "Down" was the direction towards the exterior wall, which was facing space, and "up" was the direction towards the interior wall that was closest to the core. The spaceship's multi-level, cylindrical hull with all the ship's control, living, and storage spaces rotated around the core that contained the nuclear thermal fusion reactor nicknamed "the pile," and which was the main power source for the ship. The hull and the core were separated by a sleeve of liquid hydrogen kept under a pressure of one Earth atmosphere at a temperature of 18 Kelvin, just below its boiling point of 20.28 Kelvin. The liquid hydrogen served multiple purposes. It was not only a lubricant to facilitate the rotation of the hull around the core and a source of fuel, but also served as an insulator between the hull and the core housing the photon-emitting fusion reactor.

"GM-5!" repeated the doctor as he opened the clear, multi-layered, synthetic, fused-silica cover and peered down into John's pod. "How many fingers am I holding up? Come on now, open your eyes and look. I haven't got all day. I've got to reanimate three others before chow time." The doctor was getting annoyed. "GM-5, what's with you? I'd think anyone who's been in cryo-suspension for five months would be eager to wake up. Did you really like cryo that much?" he joked. "Did you dream? GM-5!"

"Okay, okay. I'm awake…, I think." Actually, John couldn't think, but he instinctually responded just to get the doctor to quit talking. He really wanted to return to his dream.

"Three. You're holding up three fingers." *I feel like I'm coming out of a week-long, cheap-tequila bender*, he thought to himself. "Oh, my head!" he continued, whining out loud to the doctor. "It's throbbing! No one told me coming out of cryo would be like this!" *And yes,* he silently acknowledged to himself, *I was dreaming.*

"I know it's no picnic," the doctor continued to comment while making further adjustments to the cryo-pod's console. "You just lie here for about five minutes until you recover more completely. I'll go check on the others and be right back. Then, I can remove all the tubes and sensors. Don't try to get out of the cryo-pod until I return. Okay?"

"Okay," moaned John. "Don't worry about me. I'm not in any shape to go anywhere." The doctor hovered over his console for just a few seconds and then moved off to attend to the other pods that were all just a few meters away. The jungle was calling. John let himself drift back into his dream…

The six cryo-pods containing John and the five others who made up the members of the crew of colonists who were not essential for the operation of the flight itself were all situated in a single room separated only by movable screens. This was on the middle level of the spaceship's cylindrical hull's three-level structure. The first, or outside and main level, was furthest from the core and provided space for the ship's navigation, control areas, and living compartments for the working crew. Since it was the farthest from the core, it was rotating the fastest and generated the most centrifugal force. This level maintained a simulated gravity of 90% of Earth's gravity or .9 EG. The second, or middle level, provided storage space for food, parts, instruments, and any other items that were going to be frequently needed by the crew. The cryo-pods were also there. This level, being closer to the core, rotated a little more slowly than the first, outside level. The simulated gravity maintained on this level was .6 EG. The third, or inside level closest to the core, provided longer-term storage for items thought to be seldom required and for all of the materials needed specifically for establishing a colony when the ship reached its destination. These materials included the cryo-tube array preserving the human zygotes. This was the level with the largest capacity by far, and due to its proximity to the core, rotated the slowest. It maintained a simulated gravity of only .3 EG. The core itself was in the center of the ship and did not rotate. This allowed the fusion reactor to operate in a virtual, zero-gravity environment except during acceleration or deceleration. This provided more accurate controls over the level of fusion and the energy produced.

John was not at all bothered by or even aware of the .6 EG of the second level. He had fallen back to sleep and was dreaming about the jungle. The doctor, however, used the relatively low gravity to his advantage while he bounded around the cryo-pod area, back and forth from pod to pod, checking on the colonists already awakened and struggling to rouse those still asleep. One by one, the doctor was able to bring all six of the colonists out of their cryo-sleep, complete all the preliminary tests, and disconnect them from their pods. When this was done, he coaxed them out of their pods to a sitting position on the sling-chairs that hung suspended next to each pod. John just sat there staring ahead while rubbing his bald head that had been shaved in preparation for cryo-sleep. After ten minutes or so, the doctor returned to them one by one and gave them an astringent pad to wipe themselves off a bit, helped each of them into plain, white coveralls, and escorted them, again one by one, to an adjacent room. This room was empty except for molded benches jutting out of two of the walls with plenty of room for all six of them. The room itself had no other furnishings or decoration, and the benches, walls, floor, and ceiling were all the same off-white color, almost what you would call "cream." When John entered, he looked for his partner Xiaoli. At first, he couldn't find her. She was just another nondescript, completely bald person clothed in white coveralls. She recognized him before he did her and gestured slightly with a raised hand. He immediately moved to sit next to her. She welcomed him with her eyes, but they did not speak.

Xiaoli had a Chinese ancestry. She was short of stature and small-boned with straight, jet-black hair – when she had hair. She had delicate facial features with what John considered were the most amazing, almond-shaped eyes of the deepest brown. John had been first attracted to her eyes. They had met early on in the six-month-long process of screening, testing, interviewing (so many interviews!), classification, acceptance, and training to prepare them to perform their specific jobs as colonists. Even after all that, only about one in four of the original inductees made it clear through the program and survived the final cut. They were finally assigned as official "partners" after the completion of their training, and, at John's request. What was surprising, though, was that the other assembled pairs of nutritionists and civil engineers were unfamiliar to him. They were not the teams with which he and Xiaoli had trained the last couple of months before the launch. *What was going on*? he wondered.

John carried the official ID of "GM-5." "G" designated him as a "guardian," "M" identified him as male, and "5" was just a number assigned to him when he was accepted into the program. John assumed these were assigned serially and had always been proud of his relatively low number of five. Xiaoli's official ID was "GF-10." They were required to use these IDs on all official reports, but while working or off duty, they referred to each other with their given names, John and Xiaoli. Xiaoli once told him that her name means "morning Jasmine" in Chinese. She assumed all names meant something and asked him about his. He told her his name, "John," meant nothing; that English names really didn't carry any other meaning than just a name, as far as he knew. She evidently wasn't satisfied with that answer and did some research on her own and later told him that his name meant "God is Gracious." That was news to him – both that his name meant that, and that God was gracious. He'd had a pretty rough life until he had been accepted into the colonist training program.

The project was very conscientious about assigning IDs. All colonists were divided into five categories which described their general areas of expertise:

- C = Crew: The crew essential to the operation of the spaceship. They included such roles as captain, first officer, communications officer, and flight engineer.
- E = Civil Engineer: The colonists would be responsible for unloading, assembling, and maintaining all the buildings, vehicles, and tools required to support the colony.
- G = Guardian: (John and Xiaoli) The individuals responsible for attending to the human zygotes, caring

for them while they grow into embryos, fetuses, infants, and into their toddler years up through adolescence.

- N = Nutritionist: Those responsible for finding and identifying edible flora and fauna near their colony and arranging for the agricultural cultivation of all food, both native and of Earth origin.
- S = Specialist: A catch-all category for colonists with special skills. The doctor was in this category.

While the other four colonists were settling onto the benches, John, using discreet, quick glances, noted the IDs on their coveralls. They were NM-13, NF-21, EM-18, and EF-23: one pair of nutritionists and one pair of civil engineers. He wanted to ask them who they were, why they were here on this ship, and where his original colonization team members were, but they looked just as confused and disconcerted than he. The doctor had taken off his smock, and John noticed he carried the ID of SM-2. He wondered if his low serial number meant that he was one of the first doctors to be accepted into the program.

As soon as they all had taken their seats, one of the civil engineers, EM-18, asked, "Where are my partner and the other members of our colonization team? I don't recognize anyone here."

"Yes, where are our regular teams?" John asked, supporting the engineer.

The doctor hesitated and then replied, "That's something I'm neither prepared nor authorized to explain here and now. That will certainly be one of the topics at the briefing during third mess. That will happen in just a few hours. That briefing will be run by the captain and will last as long as necessary to bring you all fully up to date on our expedition and answer all your questions." The doctor shifted his position a little, "Obviously, there have been some changes in plans, but fortunately, at least in our case, they have not compromised our mission."

After his statement, he paused briefly to allow for any more comments or questions, but none came, so he gave each of them a specially prepared energy drink to reactivate their digestive systems, waited until they had finished, making sure everyone drank every drop, and then addressed them again as a group.

"Welcome back! You've all been comfortably sleeping for almost five months now while the rest of us have been slaving away running the ship," he quipped and then paused, anticipating a smile from his audience but received nothing but blank stares. "We're almost to our destination. Our ship, Ilithya-2, has been operating perfectly so far, and we are only about one Earth-week from our rendezvous with Kepler-438b. According to the schedule, it's time to wake you all up, bring you up-to-date, and allow you to orient yourself before our arrival and eventual disembarkation.

"Ilithya-2? Kepler-438b? We were scheduled for Ilithya-6 bound for the Moon! What's happened?" EM-18 again demanded.

"As I've already told you, there have been some changes in plans since you were all put into cryo-sleep. And, as I've already indicated earlier, Captain Hernandez is expecting all of you to attend the third mess tonight that will begin in something less than two hours. There, she will explain everything. In the meantime, I will show all of you to your accommodations you will use for the rest of the flight and briefly upon arrival. You'll have a short time to settle in, tidy up, and refresh yourselves. When the time comes, I'll return and escort you all to the mess hall and the captain's briefing.

"Until you get your ship legs, please be very careful while walking around," he warned. "Always use handholds wherever possible, and you will find them almost everywhere. When we go down to the first level to your quarters, you'll notice a slight increase in gravity. It may seem substantial to you and will probably make you feel very sluggish. For the next day or so, you'll tire easily until you get used to it, but you'll acclimate quickly." He paused again, allowing time for comments or questions, and then stood up and beckoned, "So, if you're ready, follow me."

John stood up, and with Xiaoli close by his side, joined the other colonists as they silently followed the doctor out of the room, down the narrow, cream-colored corridor to a stairway going down to the first level. He watched as the first couple shakily descended the staircase and paused unsteadily after reaching the bottom. "Whoa! This level does feel a lot different!" exclaimed one of the pairs. "I feel like I weigh a ton!" It wasn't until Xiaoli, and he finally did descend that he fully appreciated those comments. He gently held on to Xiaoli's arm, both for her sake and his, as they followed the doctor and the group down the first level's narrow corridor towards their quarters. He noticed that no one in the group in front of them was talking to any of the others, but then again, he realized that he and Xiaoli had barely spoken either. The shock of discovering that their entire colonization team was made up of strangers had left all of them virtually speechless.

Walking down the corridor was a strange sensation. This corridor's floor, walls, and ceiling, like the one of the second level, were all cream-colored. The floor had some textured finish on it, presumably to help with traction, but the walls and ceiling were completely smooth. In the distance, you could see that the corridor itself curved upward at a slight angle so you could only have a view about thirty meters ahead at any one time. A glance backward showed the same perspective. The floor on which they were walking was actually the exterior wall of this outermost level of the rotating hull. Although they had been exposed to a simulation of this during training, the sensation was at first a little disconcerting.

They passed many doors on both sides of the corridor on the way. These doors were of different colors: bright blue, red, yellow, or green with signs on them specifying their function. Most were closed, but a few were open and revealed medium-sized rooms containing a variety of equipment, including one which appeared to be a laundry. Since that door was opened, the sign was not visible, but the room had what looked like washing machines, and there were several plastic hampers full of rumpled white coveralls, the same as they were wearing, attached to the wall on one side. In just a few minutes, they arrived at their destination.

"Well, here it is, your 'Home, Sweet Home,' at least for the next couple of weeks or so," the doctor sang out as he directed them into a single room appearing to be about four meters by four meters with a ceiling about three meters high. The room was a duplicate of the corridor being totally cream-colored with a textured floor. There was a circular, molded table surrounded by a circular, molded, three-sectioned bench in the middle of the room that seemed to have been made out of the same material as the walls and floors. It was covered in stacks of clothing and small parcels. "Your bunks are stored in the walls and can be unfolded out like this," the doctor demonstrated by unfolding two of the bunks out of their storage compartment on one of the walls. They were stacked, one on top of the other in the manner of bunk beds. "Each of the three walls opposite the doorway has a pair of these. I recommend each team choose a wall and then decide who gets the top and who the bottom, but I'll leave all those details up to you. There are also sets of lockers on either side of the bunks for the storage of clothing and other personal items. Those items are all right there on the table. After you've chosen your locker, you can store them there. The clothing all has your IDs on them. One of those items is a plastic bottle with a drinking tube. There's a large reservoir of water fortified with electrolytes, vitamins, and some essential minerals over here by the door. Please keep yourself well-hydrated, especially over the next couple of days. Otherwise, you can situate yourselves however you like."

"This looks just like the room we spent two days in during the last part of our training," said NM-13, the male nutritionist.

"Yeah, same for me," echoed EF-23, the female civil engineer. All the others nodded in agreement. "But where's the washroom? In training, it was located behind another door, just here," she continued pointing toward an empty space next to the entry door.

"The washroom, toilets, and showers are in the room right across the corridor. Onboard the ship, we call that the 'head,' " the doctor responded. In it are two stalls for the toilets and a single large shower area, but they're all in one room. Everything's unisex here on board the ship. The location is different than your training mockup, but you should find the facilities the same. Again, I'll leave it up to you to divvy them up or segregate them as you see fit," he continued. "I'm afraid there won't be much privacy until we land, and the engineers set up our permanent quarters. Until then, we'll all just have to make do with this arrangement. It should only be for a couple weeks or so – one week until landing and one week to get everything set up – at least to a point where we can move to the new quarters." The doctor looked at each colonist and then continued, "Right now, you'll only have enough time to freshen up a little, not for showers, so get a move on."

"So, the table has our access to the computer, and the screens pop up out of the tabletop like in training?" asked Xialoi.

"Yes," the doctor confirmed, "but the screens aren't physical screens in this system. They're holograms," and with that last point, he reminded them, "I'll be back to get you in about an hour. Introduce yourselves, get to know each other a little, settle in and relax, but make sure you're all ready then."

"How will we know what time it is?" asked NF-21, the female nutritionist.

"Oh yes, there's a chronometer here on the back of the door," the doctor pointed out, pulling the door half-closed to reveal the chronometer. "I don't think that was included in your training mockup. It's digital, and the readout is the same as is used on Earth: hour, minutes, and seconds all separated by a colon. A day equals a twenty-four-hour period divided into sixty minutes divided into sixty seconds. The length of the foundation of the time, the day, is not the same length as an Earth day. It has been calibrated to equal the length of a day, a single rotation, of our new home – Kepler-438b. Its rotation time is just a little longer than the Earth's, about five hours longer. As a result, your time estimates will be a little off for a while. For example, five Kepler-438b minutes are the same as six Earth minutes. That should help all of you who have a bad habit of being late all the time," he joked, but his effort at humor again fell flat. He thought to himself, his jokes might not be working well because the timing was off (a meta-joke) and chuckled to himself, but then just continued on with his explanation.

"Also, it's ship-time, not Earth-time, but all that will be explained to you at the briefing," he added mischievously. "It's now 17:35, and third-mess is at 18:00. I'll be back at 17:55 to escort you. That's twenty minutes ship-time or a little over twenty-four minutes Earth-time. Any more questions?" There being none, the doctor left the room, closing the door behind him.

The female nutritionist spoke first, "I hope someone understood all that time stuff because I sure didn't." For a few seconds, the group just stood and stared at each other.

The male civil engineer looked at everyone and blurted out to no one in particular, "Just what the hell do you think is going on?" No one replied.

John moved over to the table, sat down, and rummaged through the clothes until he found the stack marked with his ID, GM-5. He put his arms around this and pushed the rest of the clothes and packets more into the middle of the table. Xiaoli did likewise. "I have absolutely no idea," he finally responded, "And, by the way, my name is John."

"And I'm Xiaoli. We're the guardian team."

One by one, the others took seats and started searching through the piles for their clothes.

"My name is Gagandeep," the man sitting next to John said. He was a short, thin-faced, dark-skinned Indian. "I'm a nutritionist.

"I'm his partner, Waniratanakanya. I don't know why Thai names are so long," she added with a laugh. "You can just call me 'Wan.' " She was also petite with dark skin.

The man directly across from John seemed very agitated and announced, "I'm Malcolm and a civil engineer, but I've never met this woman who I assume is to be my partner." Malcolm was of stocky build, like a bodybuilder, medium height, and spoke with an Australian accent.

"I'm Zawadi," the woman sitting next to him offered while giving Malcolm a disapproving stare. Zawadi was a Black woman, slender, and very tall, probably every bit of two meters. She had an air of authority about her.

"How did we all get here, on this ship, with this mix of teams?" Malcolm continued his interrogation.

"I have no idea," offered John. "The last thing I remember was being put into the cryo-tube to be delivered to the Ilithya-2, which I thought was bound for Ganymede, one of Jupiter's moons, with the rest of our teams. Then, I woke up here to all of this." John didn't mention his dreams. Everyone nodded in agreement. "It's a mystery and one which I don't think we're going to be able to solve ourselves. We're just going to have to wait on the captain's briefing like the doctor said." He turned to Xiaoli as he continued, "So, I think Xia and I are just going to check out our bunk and lockers and try to settle in and wait for the briefing.

"That sounds like a good plan," agreed Zawadi, but her new partner Malcolm did not seem to agree.

"Let's see what we can find on the computer about all this," Malcolm suggested. With that, he seated himself on one of the bench sections, stared at the table and barked his command, "Computer, raise my screen." Nothing happened. He tried again, "Computer, raise my screen. Computer, do you read me?" Again, no response.

"Maybe we don't have voice authorization to use the

computer yet. How could we? This is not the ship or the computer, or even the mission to which we were originally assigned," Zawadi suggested.

"Computer!" Malcolm repeated again and again. In the meantime, the rest of the group moved to their bunks and lockers and began to settle in. After more than just a few further unsuccessful attempts, Malcolm reluctantly joined them.

When the different pairs were done puttering around their bunk and locker stations, they all reassembled at the center table. Malcolm made a few more attempts to arouse the computer until he was told to, "Just knock it off!" by his exasperated partner Zawadi. Except for these two civil engineers who sat in silence, the rest of the teams talked quietly to each other, and every now and then, some muted laughter could be heard.

Precisely at 17:55 hours by the chronometer on the back of the door, the doctor reappeared as promised. "Well, boys and girls, we're off to see the wizard!" he quipped, again drawing not a hint of a smile from anyone. "Don't you all want to know just what kind of rabbit hole you've fallen into?" Still nothing, so he continued in a more serious tone, "No need to take anything. The entire briefing will be recorded and available in the computer's video library."

"We can't seem to access the computer," complained Malcolm.

"Yes, well...none of you have been voice-printed yet and given access. Everything in due time," the doctor intoned in a singsong voice and a wry smile, "Everything in due time."

And with that, the doctor stood up, exited through the door, and led the group down the corridor to the mess hall.

Chapter 2

Welcome Aboard

The mess hall was only a little larger than their quarters. It was the same width, about four meters, but probably twice as long, about eight meters. It, like all the rooms they had seen so far, was entirely cream-colored with a textured floor. The mess hall had four circular tables with benches exactly like the ones in their cabin. There were four people already in the room, and it looked like they had been waiting on them. All were clothed in the same white coveralls as theirs. Three people were already seated at two of the far tables, two at one table and one at the other. One person, a woman, was standing behind the tables just to the side of a holographic projection that seemed to emanate out of the back wall. She was chatting with the man seated alone at the table nearest her. She stopped talking when the colonists entered, waited for them to get settled, and then began, "Project Sixth Day," she announced with a gesture of her hand toward the hologram.

The projection had the logo of Project Sixth Day at the top and projected the following text:

Logo - Project Sixth Day

Genesis 1:27-31

[27]God created man in His own image, in the image of God He created him; male and female He created them. [28]God blessed them; and God said to them, "Be fruitful and multiply, and fill the earth, and subdue it; and rule over the fish of the sea and over the birds of the sky and over every living thing that moves on the earth..." [31]And there was evening, and there was morning, the sixth day.

The doctor faced the colonists and directed them to, "Take a seat anywhere," gesturing towards two tables nearest the door which had drink glasses on them. He then continued on forward to stand next to the woman at the back of the room. "The glasses contain some liquid nutrient for you. It's what you need right now to give you some energy and also begin restarting your digestive system. This will be your diet for the next two days, so get used to it." He waited until they all sat down and then continued, "This is Captain Beatrice Hernandez. You may address her as 'Captain.' She will be conducting your

'Welcome Aboard' briefing today that will bring you up-to-date on the status of Project Sixth Day, our mission, and hopefully be able to answer all your questions." With that, the doctor sat down, and the captain stepped forward.

"Yes, welcome aboard. Actually, you've all already been aboard for about five months, ship-time, or over seven-hundred years Earth-time." This brought an audible gasp from the colonists. They exchanged furtive glances at each other and shifted nervously on their benches. The captain definitely had their attention now.

"Where to start? I think I'll start by introducing the rest of our crew. To my extreme right is First Officer Gary Butler." The first officer raised his hand in acknowledgment. "Gary should be your first point of contact on any issues regarding the operation of this ship. You should address him as 'First Officer' or 'Mr. Butler.'

"Next to him is Flight Engineer Hokolequa. That's his American Indian name, Shawnee, to be specific. We all just call him 'Hoke,' and you may too. He knows everything there is to know about the mechanical, electrical, hydraulic, you-name-it, systems on the ship, including the operation of the thermonuclear fusion reactor.

"Next, of course, is someone you've already met, Dr. Ian MacTavish."

The doctor raised his hand and added, "You can call me anything you'd like, but just don't call me late for dinner," he tried joking again — and again was unsuccessful.

"Finally, there is Lyuba Alkaev, our cyberneticist. She takes care of all of our control systems, including our robots and, perhaps most important to you over the next week and from now on, our computer. After this meeting, depending on how long we go, she will want to meet with you all in your quarters and formally introduce you to Ana, our central computer. I'll cover as much as I can in this briefing, but I'm sure there will be many things on which you'll want more details. You should be able to find them on Ana. Now, it's your turn. Please tell us your ID, name — first name is sufficient — and function; and reply by team, please."

Zawadi immediately led off, "I'm EF-23, Zawadi, a civil engineer.

"I'm Malcolm, EM-18, civil engineer, but Zawadi is not my original team member."

"We know there have been reassignments," acknowledged the captain. "We'll get into all that later." She looked at the next colonist and said, "Please continue."

"I'm Gagandeep, NM-13, nutritionist."

"I'm the other nutritionist. My ID is NF-21, and my name is Waniratanakanya," then Wan added softly, "But you can just call me 'Wan.' "

"John, here, GM-5, guardian."

"I am Xiaoli," Xiaoli said with a respectful bow of her head, "GF-10, guardian."

The introductions now complete, the captain began the briefing, "Okay, so, as has been hinted, there's been some changes in the original plans — actually, some major changes. As you all already know Project Sixth Day," she gestured to the hologram, "was the brainchild of a carefully selected group of scientists and sociologists at the behest of a cabal of the highest level of ministers in our One World Government. The world was on what was perceived as an increasingly dangerous course from a combination of continuing and escalating overpopulation, insurgent military actions, and environmental pollution. In spite of the best efforts of the One World Government, none of these calamities were seen likely to be brought under control in the then foreseeable future. The end had been feared for some time now.

To prepare for that end, for over twenty years, space projects had been developed, launched, and conducted to learn how to best build habitats for humans, and find alternate planets on which to relocate the human race – at least relocate a selected few. These programs had started with experimental habitats in space, first, orbiting the Earth, then several on the Moon, and finally, one very large project on Mars. All of these projects achieved some success, but the final results were always mixed, and the downside was always the same: none of the habitats could be developed to be self-sustaining, at least not for very long. The reason, of course, was that the external environments in which these habitats were built could not support human life without a tremendous amount of artificial environment support – and more problematic, direct support from Earth. You were all part of Project Sixth Day's missions to continue the development and improvements of the habitats, so a substantial number could be built on a planet or planets that could support human life without relying on continuing support from Earth. This, however, was just the short-term objective of Project Sixth Day, the first phase."

Again, there were some nervous murmurings among the colonists.

The captain took a drink of water, looked around the room, particularly at her assembled crew, and then continued, "In the early twenty-first century, there were already projects underway to identify potentially habitable exoplanets – planets outside of the Solar System. One of the earliest organized programs was one sponsored by an organization called NASA in a historical nation-state called the United States of America. The project was popularly known as the 'Goldilocks Project,' referring to an ancient fable." The captain then addressed the computer, "Ana, Goldilocks Fable please," and immediately, the Project Sixth Day hologram dissolved into one with a quaint drawing and the following quote from the fable...

Goldilocks Doctrine

"This porridge is too hot!" Goldilocks exclaimed. So, she tasted the porridge from the second bowl.
 "This porridge is too cold," so, she tasted the last bowl of porridge.
 "Ahhh, this porridge is just right!" she said happily.

"...in which a girl named Goldilocks samples bowls of porridge trying to find one that is not too hot and not too cold, but just right. This 'just right' quality was the same kind of quality the scientists were looking for to find habitable exoplanets. Hot and cold were important, but they were certainly not the only factors that needed to be considered. The scientists made up an entire matrix of criteria that they thought were among the fundamental qualities any planet, or other heavenly body, would need to have to support human life. These changed over time. Criteria were added and subtracted, but finally, they settled on a critical few.

"The Goldilocks Project expanded and finally was split

up, but one of the most successful spinoffs was the work done mainly at NASA's Kepler Space Telescope and the creation of a compilation of Goldilocks-class exoplanets called the *Habitable Exoplanets Catalog*. NASA astronomers constantly scoured the heavens looking for likely candidates. In the end, they were successful beyond anyone's wildest dreams. The catalog eventually listed hundreds of 'Goldilocks-class' exoplanets that had been scrupulously documented after being evaluated on seven different criteria."

The captain then turned and motioned at the Goldilocks's holographic image and remarked, "That was then, but this is now. Ana," she commanded, "display the seven criteria used to build the *Habitable Exoplanets Catalog*." Immediately, the holographic image of the Goldilocks Fable dissolved and was replaced with a page of text so long it extended from the ceiling almost to the floor:

Habitable Exoplanets Catalog

Criteria Definitions

1. **Earth Similarity Index (ESI)** – Similarity to Earth on a scale from 0 to 1, with 1 being the most Earth-like. ESI depends on the planet's radius, density, escape velocity, and surface temperature.
2. **Standard Primary Habitability (SPH)** – Suitability for vegetation on a scale from 0 to 1, with 1 being best-suited for growth. SPH depends on surface temperature (and relative humidity if known).

3. **Habitable Zone Distance (HZD)** – Distance from the center of the star's habitable zone, scaled so that −1 represents the inner edge of the zone, and +1 represents the outer edge. HZD depends on the star's luminosity and temperature and the size of the planet's orbit.

4. **Habitable Zone Composition (HZC)** – Measure of bulk composition, where values close to zero are likely iron–rock–water mixtures. Values below −1 represent bodies likely composed mainly of iron, and values greater than +1 represent bodies likely composed mainly of gas. HZC depends on the planet's mass and radius.

5. **Habitable Zone Atmosphere (HZA)** – Potential for the planet to hold a habitable atmosphere, where values below −1 represent bodies likely with little or no atmosphere, and values above +1 represent bodies likely with thick hydrogen atmospheres (e.g. gas giants). Values between −1 and +1 are more likely to have atmospheres suitable for life, though zero is not necessarily ideal. HZA depends on the planet's mass, radius, orbit size, and the star's luminosity.

6. **Planetary Class (pClass)** – Classifies objects based on thermal zone (hot, warm, or cold, where warm is in the habitable zone) and mass (asteroidean, mercurian, subterran, terran, superterran, neptunian, and jovian).

7. **Habitable Class (hClass)** – Classifies habitable planets based on temperature: hypopsychroplanets (hP) = very cold (< –50 °C); psychroplanets (P) = cold; mesoplanets (M) = medium-temperature (0–50 °C; not to be confused with the other definition of mesoplanets); thermoplanets (T) = hot; hyperthermoplanets (hT) = very hot (> 100 °C). Mesoplanets would be ideal for complex life, whereas class hP or hT would only support extremophilic life. Non-habitable planets are simply given the class NH.

The captain only gave the group about a minute to scan through the hologram and then said, "All this is accessible via Ana, so don't try to take it all in right now. The important thing to take away is the search for habitable planets takes a lot more than just 'not too hot and not too cold' into consideration. A lot of thought and work went into these studies to give us the very best candidates for the longer-term objective of Project Sixth Day: the establishment of self-sustaining colonies that would not be tied to habitats in which an artificial environment would have to be maintained. This was the long-term objective of Project Sixth Day, the final phase.

"You were all trained as part of Phase I, and I know were expecting to join your other team members on board one of ten spaceships scheduled to establish advanced technology habitats on moons or planets within the Solar System. The Phase I missions consisted of the establishment of two additional habitats on the Moon, six at various sites on Mars, and two unique subterranean habitats on Ganymede, the largest of the four Galileanclass moons of Jupiter. Project Sixth Day had built and readied ten spaceships of a new design – the Ilithya class. These are the ships on whose mockups you were trained. One of the most important innovations in the Ilithya class ships was their thrust source. It was powered by the usual fusion reactor, but the propulsion system was of a new, top-secret design: a pulse, Z-boson engine which was capable of near-light speeds. The latest tweaks and tests projected a theoretical limit of as much as ninety-five percent of the speed of light, or Tal 95."

This was beginning to be all too much for Malcolm to take in, "What's 'Tal' stand for?" he interrupted.

" 'Tal' is a term used to define speeds approaching the speed of light. It is analogous to the term 'Mach,' which is used to compare speeds to the speed of sound," the captain started patiently explaining. " 'Tal' is the ratio of the speed of an object moving through a vacuum and the speed of light. Ana, display the formula for Tal." Ana dutifully dissolved the large *Habitable Exoplanets Catalog* hologram and replaced it with the formula for calculating Tal:

Formula for Calculating Tal Number

$$T = (v_{object} / v_{light}) \times 100$$

where:

T is the Tal number, a whole number representing a percentage of the speed of light.

Ex. Tal 30 = 0.3 C or 30% C.

v_{object} is the velocity of the source relative to the medium, and

v_{light} is the speed of light in the medium (C in a vacuum).

Malcolm just stared numbly at the hologram, shook his head slightly, and muttered something inaudible.

" 'Tal' is short for 'Talaria,' which are the winged sandals of the Greek god Hermes or the Roman god Mercury," added the first officer. "The term 'Mach,' of course, was named after a historical scientist named 'Ernst Mach.' Ana will help you find all this and much more historical and explanatory information about things like these – after Lyuba sets up your profiles, that is."

The captain moved forward, right up to the front of the colonists' tables. "So far, I've pretty much told you most everything you already know, although I probably went into a little more detail than you were given in your training. Now, it's time to tell you about the changes in plans." She moved back to her place at the back of the room. "Do you want a break first, before we continue?"

The colonists all looked at each other but were silent until Zawadi finally spoke for them all, "No, that's not necessary. We want to know everything. We want to know everything now."

"Fine," continued the captain. "In that case, we'll start the day you were all put into cryo-suspension in anticipation of your boarding the ships for your various missions. Do you all remember that?"

"I do," offered Gagandeep, "and that's the last thing I remember."

All of the others nodded in agreement, except John. *I remember that, sure, but I also remember the dreams – the dreams about the jungle*, he thought to himself. *I wonder if the others had dreams too, and what they were about. I'll have to ask Xia...*

"Yes, you were all put into cryo-suspension and made ready to be transported to your ships." The captain paused, looked at her crew for support, and then announced, "It was then the first attack came."

"Attack! What do you mean 'attack?' Who would attack us?" Malcolm asked incredulously.

"As you all know, there had been sporadic but continual attacks on various government buildings and areas by the insurgents. Up to then, though, the attacks had been relatively small operations involving only a handful of insurgents, outdated and ineffective equipment, and mainly just improvised explosive devices and small arms. This attack was different and would change not only the project but the course of the entire world dramatically." The colonists all sat with their attention riveted upon her.

"This attack was accomplished by their hacking into two, decommissioned, military satellites with laser-artillery capability. The technology onboard was obsolete, and their orbits had decayed enough to be considered ineffective. The One World Military had disabled them, and they were scheduled for eventual destruction. The insurgents, some say with the help of traitors within our own military, were able to hack into these two satellites' control systems and reactivate their laser weapons. They had learned of Project Sixth Day's objectives and suspected if, and when the project succeeded, only those in league with the One World Government would be relocated to alternate worlds, and they would be left there on Earth to clean up the mess.

They chose the spaceship port that was housing Project Sixth Day's ten Ilithya-class spaceships. Their two-pronged attack completely destroyed two ships, damaged five severely, and three others to a lesser extent. The attack also targeted some of the project's buildings, and one was...," the captain paused slightly before delivering this news she knew would be very distressing to the colonists, "...the lab and hospital building housing all your cryo-pods."

The colonists erupted in first an audible gasp and then scattered cries of, "No!"

"What?"

"Why the lab and hospital?"

"Were there casualties?"

"Yes, I can understand your anger. It's one thing to destroy some spaceships and even the entire spaceport, but why the medical lab?" the captain commiserated. "We don't know. We don't know if the medical lab was a mistake, some say it was. In fact, the official insurgent statement after the attack said it was, but most of us believe it was purposeful. They just wanted to cause as much destruction, loss of life, and misery as they could, as they usually intend to do." The captain went on speaking slowly and deliberately, "Yes, there were casualties, many of them.

"There were enough colonists there in cryo for the ten spaceships: ten teams of six each, just like are assembled here, sixty in total. Out of the sixty, thirty-two were killed outright, and twelve pods sustained so much damage that ten of their occupants died within days. The other two survived for a week or so, but were in so much pain, eventually requested euthanasia. The damage done to a human body expelled abruptly from cryo-suspension is pretty horrendous. It's not something I will ever forget or ever want to see again."

The colonists shuffled a little on their benches but wanted her to continue. "What about my original partner, EM-16?" Zawadi enquired softly. "Is he dead?"

"I don't know all the details about every casualty. You can research that later with Ana if you wish. I only know were just sixteen survivors, and, of course, you were among them."

"Sixteen?" wailed Wan. "Only sixteen survivors? Why weren't we then immediately brought out of cryo-sleep?"

"Right after the attack was quashed and the two rogue satellites destroyed, the sixteen ministers of the High Council of the One World Government convened and, of course, ordered damage reports. While they were being compiled, which took about a week, the High Council had already come to the conclusion that there was now a real danger of complete destruction and the eventual extinction of the human species, along with probably more than half of the life on Earth. They were ready to make the decision to not only continue with Project Sixth Day, but to accelerate it. Once they had the damage reports, they ordered the project to move immediately to Phase II, the colonization of habitable exoplanets.

"As a result of that acceleration order and after plotting out a timeline, it was decided to keep all of you in cryo-suspension for the time being. It was estimated that the three, only slightly damaged ships could be repaired and refitted for the new missions in about three months. It ended up taking six months, but in the end, the three ships were repaired, enhanced with the new, pulse, Z-boson thrust sources, rechristened as Ilithya-1, -2, and -3, finally pronounced ready to go and moved again to the launch pads. In the meantime, the surviving sixteen of you were assigned new partners, where necessary, and shuffled around into new teams. The results were that Ilithya-1 and Ilithya-2 were fitted out with a full complement of six-colonist teams, whereas Ilithya-3 was only assigned four colonists: two civil engineers, one guardian, and one nutritionist. There was talk of delaying Ilithya-3 until two more colonists could be trained, but by that time, the threat from the insurgents and the deteriorating condition of the Earth warranted going ahead with the reduced team.

The launch date was set, and crews and teams were loaded aboard. Ilithya-1 departed Earth in the early morning hours of June 22, 2149. We, on Ilithya-2, followed the next day, and Ilithya-3 the morning after that. So, that's how you all ended up here."

There being no questions, she continued. "After we achieved Earth orbit and ran through our extensive checklist, Ana plotted our course to slingshot around the Sun. After three Earth orbits, we started the first part of our journey. We arrived in close orbit around the Sun thirty-two days later and used two solar orbits to build up momentum to slingshot us towards our final destination."

"Our destination?" queried Malcolm, "And just where is that?"

"For once, I'm glad you asked that question," the captain quipped, only half-jokingly, "Our mission was fortunate enough to be assigned one of the very best habitable exoplanet candidates: Kepler-438b.

"Ana, Kepler-438 system please," the captain requested, and a hologram appeared of a small, reddish star being orbited by five planets. The hologram projected the star in the middle of the room, and the planets' orbits extended to the walls on the narrow side.

"This is the red dwarf star Kepler-438. It is in the constellation Lyra. It was discovered in the mid-twentieth century but wasn't seen as having a great significance until 2015 when Kepler-438b, the second planet nearest the star in this system, was discovered.

"Ana, Kepler-438b criteria compared with Earth and Mars, please." The hologram changed to a textual list. "Kepler-438b was quickly identified as a Goldilocks-class exoplanet, and, through further telescopic and radiographic readings, was determined to look very promising indeed." The captain motioned to the new display, "Its scores on the seven criteria of the Habitable Exoplanet Catalog indexing scheme compared with Earth, and contrasted with Mars, are very impressive:"

Comparison Chart of Kepler-438b, Earth & Mars

Criteria	Kepler-438b	Earth	Mars
ESI Earth Similarity Index	0.88	1.00	0.64
SPH Standard Primary Habitability	0.88	0.72	0.00
HZD Habitable Zone Distance	-0.93	-0.59	+0.33
HZC Habitable Zone Composition	-0.14	-0.31	-0.13
HZA Habitable Zone Atmosphere	-0.73	-0.52	-1.12
pClass Planetary Class	warm terran	warm terran	warm terran
hClass Habitable Class	meso-planet	meso-planet	hypo-phsychro-planet

"See how close Kepler-438b matches Earth criteria? It's almost miraculous," the captain pointed out.

After a few ooh's and aah's, and several, short hushed private discussions among the colonists the captain continued, "Ana, Kepler-438b details," barked the captain, and immediately a detailed holographic chart showing the physical characteristics of Kepler-438b spread across the back wall:

Kepler-438b Physical Characteristics

Kepler-438b

Approximate size comparison of Kepler-438b (right) with Earth

Physical characteristics

Radius	(r)	1.120 $R_\oplus$
Stellar flux	($F_\odot$)	1.38 $\oplus$
Temperature	(T)	273 K (0 °C; 32 °F)

Orbital elements

Semi-major axis	(a)	0.16600 AU
Eccentricity	(e)	0.03 (+0.01, −0.03)
Orbital period	(P)	35.23319000
Rotational period	(R)	1.2046800
Inclination	(i)	89.860°

"That, colonists, is our mission's destination: Kepler-438b. And, it will be our new home." She let that statement hang in the air for a while.

She allowed the colonists to talk amongst themselves. When they'd seemed to come to some closure or consensus, they broke their huddles and turned around to face the captain. Zawadi kept her seat but again spoke for them all, "Many of the things you've told us are distressing, but we understand most of them. One of the most problematic points, however, is the distance this planet is from Earth. We assume since it is an exoplanet, it is outside of the Solar System, but you didn't tell us how far away it was. We think you said it was orbiting a star in a constellation...did you say 'Lyra'?"

"Yes," the captain interrupted. "...Lyra. We can discuss that now. Kepler-438 is, itself, a "red dwarf." That's a relatively cool star. They are the most common stars in our section of the universe and make up as many as three-quarters of the stars in the Milky Way. The reason they are less luminous is that they are fully convective, so the helium produced by the fusion reaction is completely recirculated instead of discharged, which prolongs the fusion period. They develop more slowly than other, brighter stars, and actually last longer. "

"If it's not very bright, how can its planets support life?" questioned Malcolm."

It can, in Kepler-438b's case, because it is much closer to this star than Earth is to the Sun," the captain replied. "Ana, project the details on Kepler-438."

Kepler-438 Physical Characteristics

Star		Kepler-438
sClass		Red Dwarf
Constellation		Lyra
Right Ascension	(α)	$18^h\ 46^m\ 35.000^s$
Declination	(δ)	$+41°\ 57'\ 3.93''$
Apparent Magnitude	(m_V)	14.467
Distance		475 ly (145 pc)
Mass	(m)	0.540 $M_\odot$
Radius	(r)	0.520 $R_\odot$
Temperature	(T)	3748 K
Metallicity	[Fe/H]	0.160
Age		4.4 (+0.8, −0.7) Gyr

"If I'm reading this correctly, it says the star Kepler-438 is four hundred seventy-five light-years from Earth!" John exclaimed.

"Yes, you're reading it right," acknowledged the captain.

"Four hundred seventy-five light-years? But how could that be?" John continued incredulously. Then he asked accusingly, "Where are we? What have you done?"

An uncomfortable silence hovered over the room. All the colonists were looking first at the captain and then the crew, their eyes begging for answers.

"You're right, four hundred seventy-five light-years, or one-hundred and forty-five parsecs. However you state it, it's a long, long way, but actually not as long a distance as either Ilithya-1's or Ilithya-3's destinations, actually, almost half of theirs..., if that little bit of information helps any."

"No, it doesn't help me at all!" John angrily exclaimed. "But how could that be? When I was awakened from cyro-sleep, I was told we were only about a week from our destination. Do you mean to tell me that we've gone four hundred seventy-five light-years, minus one week, since we embarked?"

"Yes. That's exactly what I mean to tell you."

"But how?" John moaned.

"By traveling at near-light speed. I told you the new Ilithya-class spaceships had been equipped with state-of-the-art, pulse, Z-boson-thrust sources which have that capability, theoretically." She paused for a few seconds and then added, "Well, I guess I could now confidently say that's not just theory anymore. It's a fact."

"So, you're telling me we've traveled four hundred and seventy-five light-years on this ship? On this ship right here? And we're now only a week from Kepler...whatever?" John dug at her again.

"Yes. That's what I'm saying. Are you hearing me?"

All the colonists slumped back on their benches and exchanged worrying glances at one another. Most were just too overwhelmed to speak, but not Malcolm.

"Do you mean we've been on this ship in cryo-sleep for four hundred and seventy-five years?"

"Not exactly...Let me explain. Ana, project the relevant Lorentz equations, including the four-vectors and the Mikowski metric... No, belay that," she suddenly added. "This meeting is running a lot longer than I allotted, and you can research all that on your own time. I'll just give you the layman's version.

"The theory of special relativity is based on the assumption, now accepted as indisputable fact, that the speed of light is a universal, physical constant. That means no matter where you are, or how fast you are moving, or which direction you are going, if you measure the speed of light in a vacuum, it will always result in a velocity of 299,792,458 meters per second. That's an exact measurement because, in fact, way back in 1983, we redefined the meter so it would exactly conform with this measurement. It doesn't matter if the light is coming at you or going away from you – whether it is coming straight on, at right angles, or at any other vector. These are all explained and can be calculated by the Lorentz and other relativistic equations that Ana will be glad to walk you through.

"Apparent velocity, or the measurement of relative speed, is a ratio of distance over time. An example would be if you're traveling in a vehicle going fifty kilometers per hour, and you are approaching a car in front of you that is going the same way as you but at forty kilometers per hour, it would measure your apparent speed, the speed relative to it, at only ten kilometers per hour. If, however, the same vehicle was coming directly at you at the same forty kilometers per hour, you would measure its apparent speed at ninety kilometers per hour.

"Since, however, the speed of light is an absolute, a universal constant, it will always be measured the same. So, if you take that same scenario, but the object in front of you and the object coming at you were traveling at the speed of light, the speeds of both objects will always give you the exactly same measurement – the speed of light."

The colonists were all trying very hard to follow her explanation.

"That means that the relative variables in this equation, when applied to the speed of light, are time and distance. In other words, instead of the apparent velocity of an object changing relative to your velocity, the time for you, or the distance traveled, have to be the variable. The apparent velocity of light is the constant.

"The corollary is: 'as an object approaches the speed of light, time and distance approach zero;' or to put it more simply and apply it to our spaceship, as our ship travels at near-light speed, time on the ship slows down and distance is foreshortened. This slowing down of time and foreshortening of distance is, of course, all relative to some other object and not something measurable on the object itself, such as our spaceship. The speed of light is always a constant, and it is our measurement of time and distance that has to vary."

"That's an oversimplification," objected Hoke, the flight engineer. He stood up behind his table and started lecturing, "It's true that the measurement of the speed of light is always constant, and it's time and distance that are relative, but in point of fact, time and distance are just two sides of the same coin. To say time slows or distance foreshortens is like me claiming that I'm taller than you, but you disagreeing by claiming you're shorter than me. Time and distance are all part of the space-time continuum."

"Yes," interrupted the captain, "but they can research all that with Ana. I don't want to get hung up on that here. It's as bad as arguing over religion."

Hoke reluctantly sat back down, but not before he gave the captain a disapproving stare and added, "It's not either time or distance. They're the same thing. It's both."

"Captain, with all due respect, you still haven't answered my question," pressed John. "How long have we been on this ship?"

The captain looked John up and down, carefully measuring him as if to see if she could detect an attitude of defiance. "You have been on this ship in cryo-suspension since you were loaded aboard. That was a little less than six months ago..." The mood of the colonists in the room lightened a bit, until she added, "...ship-time."

"Ship-time? What do you mean 'ship-time?' " John shot back.

" 'Ship-time' is the time on the ship," she replied matter-of-factly. "I just explained to you time was relative, and ship-time is the time relative to the ship."

"What other time is there?" asked John cautiously. He felt a growing coldness in the pit of his stomach. He was not sure if he really wanted an answer or not.

"There're lots of other time frames, an infinite number, in fact, but I assume what you're digging for is an answer in 'Earth-time.' "

"Yes, that's what I want," John agreed. "How long have we been on this ship in 'Earth-time?' "

The room was completely still. All eyes were riveted on the captain. She cleared her throat, glanced at her crew seeking their support, and reluctantly replied, "Six-hundred and fifty years – a little over six-hundred fifty years Earth-time."

No one said a word. No one even moved. All the colonists just sat at their places and stared straight ahead. The captain finally broke the awkward silence with, "I think this meeting is over. The doctor will escort you back to your quarters. I'll instruct Lyuba to come visit you at 08:00, or in about ten hours, escort you to first mess, and then set you all up with computer access. Talk among yourselves. Get some sleep. Take long showers. Try to relax. Everything is going as well as it can, and better than anyone expected."

With that, her crew stood up, and she and they filed silently out of the mess hall, and each turning their own way, disappeared down the corridor.

The doctor then got up and moved to the door. "Follow me," he offered. "I'll walk with you to your quarters.

Oh yes, and..." he added with more than a little hint of sarcasm, "...welcome aboard!"

Chapter 3

Reorientation

When the colonists arrived back at their quarters, there was no group discussion concerning the briefing. That wasn't because there was nothing to discuss, but because there was too much. They were all overwhelmed. They quickly split up into their pairings, each pair retreating to their separate bunk areas.

Gagandeep and Wan pulled down and sat on their lower bunk talking quietly. Wan was visibly upset, softly sobbing at times and leaning over on Gagandeep seeking comfort. Gagandeep didn't really have much to say but sat stoically staring out into the center of the room. After about thirty minutes, he patted her hand, got up, and pulled down the upper bunk in preparation for retiring.

Zawadi and Malcolm were a different story entirely. When they got to their bunk area, they had a hushed but virulent fight over just who would sleep in which bunk. They both wanted the lower bunk, and neither seemed like they would yield. Malcolm finally did capitulate and abruptly jerked down the upper bunk, but not before he got off a few choice words. While he was berating her, Zawadi moved to claim the rightmost locker. Malcolm started to protest, but she quickly pointed her finger at him, stared him square in the eye, and hissed, "Don't you start again, now!" and continued to store her clothes and personal items in the locker.

John and Xia first went to their bunk areas and pulled down their bunks, checked out their lockers, but then moved to sit at the table in the center of the room. After they were seated, John turned to Xia and asked, "How are you doing?"

Xia looked at him and just nodded her head slightly, indicating that she was okay. John was then reminded of how much he was constantly amazed by Xia's eyes. They were simply mesmerizing. Right now, they seemed to be reaching out to him, searching for answers to make some sense out of what they'd just sat through. They stared at each other for a few moments until Xia finally spoke, "What do you think happened to the rest of our team? Lars, Maria, Ai, …"

"Stop!" commanded John. "There's no use in dwelling on them right now. We can find all that out tomorrow after we're set up with computer access, but I do think if they were all alive and still together, they'd be with us here, on this team, on this ship. Why would they split us up further?" John reasoned.

Xia's eyes filled, first with sadness, but that slowly transformed into resignation, "Yes, you're right. We can find out tomorrow – for all the good that will do," she added with a shrug. "Did you understand everything that was presented to us in the briefing?

"No! Hell no! I was following it okay up until she started talking about light speed, and ship-time and Earth-time. Then everything just seemed to go by like a blur, and her explanations were only a 'wah-wah-wah' in the background. I have no idea what she said or how that really affects us, but I have this feeling that it's not good," John exclaimed. "What do you think? You're the one with the eerily accurate intuition, not me. What do you think?"

"I think... I mean, I feel... I feel it's bad too. In fact, I feel like we've just been pushed off a precipice and into a bottomless chasm, and we're all in freefall — disoriented and completely helpless." Xia lowered her head and stared blankly at the tabletop. "What are we going to do?"

John thought he should try to lighten the mood up a little bit and quickly moved to change the subject, "Well, there's nothing we can do about all that tonight, so let's get cleaned up and hit the sack. What do you say? All this freefalling has made me sleepy," he joked, trying to pry out a smile from his partner. It worked.

"Okay, that's probably a good idea. I like it. I'm ready," and with, that Xia got up, turned to wait for John, and then together, they both moved to their bunks and prepared for bed.

* * * *

John lay quietly on his back in the jungle on the soft moss floor by the edge of a slow-moving stream. His eyes were half-closed, and his ears were filled with the soothing sound of the water rippling over the shallow bed. The shifting light filtering down through the gently moving trees seemed to be synchronized with the stream's song. He slowly rolled on his side to view the singing water. It flowed slowly enough that the forest canopy was mirrored on its surface, but fast enough to distort the images so they would dance and shimmer. He lay this way for a time, and then, in his dream, he closed his eyes and quickly fell into a deep, silent sleep.

* * * *

"Knock, knock...," called Lyuba softly, the ship's cyberneticist, as she opened the door and entered their quarters. "Rise and shine!" she continued a little louder. "First mess will begin in about fifteen minutes, so you better get a move on if you want a nice yummy glass of the doctor's liquid nutrient," she made a face and then laughed. "You'll have to put up with it for the rest of the day, so I'm told, but tomorrow, you'll be able to join the rest of us in some real food. It's not 'real' real food, actually, but it looks and tastes like real food. At least it's solid food and not 'liquid nutrients,' " she made a face again and then said, "I'll pop back in here in a while and shepherd you all down to the mess. After we eat, we can come back here and get started with your formal introductions to Ana." With that, she closed the door.

"Fifteen minutes? Are those Earth-minutes, ship-minutes, or Kepler-whatever minutes?" asked Malcolm sarcastically.

"It really doesn't matter," Zawadi said with some exasperation in her voice. "All that should mean to you is that you better not drag your ass around this morning."

Malcolm bristled and immediately dove into his locker and grabbed a towel and a new set of coveralls. "I'm taking a quick shower," he informed Zawadi. Do you want to join me to make sure I wash behind my ears? We could then make it a long shower," he jabbed at her.

"No, thanks," she immediately countered. "I don't want to spoil my breakfast. I'll wait until after I eat."

John started to join Malcolm, but Gagandeep beat him to it. "I'll join you," he said and walked with Malcolm across the hall to the head and shower area. John remained behind and began organizing his locker.

Not long after Malcolm and Gagandeep returned and dressed, Lyuba reappeared and led them all down the corridor to the mess. The four tables with benches were still there and in the same place. John noted this, but then realized they would always be in the same place because they were molded into the floor. The first officer and the flight engineer were sitting at one of the back tables but were just getting up to leave when the colonists entered. They both smiled and nodded at the colonists on their way out, but nothing was said. There was no sign of the captain. There were six glasses of nutritional liquid sitting on the first two tables, the same tables they had sat at for the "Welcome Aboard" briefing. Lyuba went to the back of the room to a window, got a tray of food, "real" food, and returned to sit with them.

"Well now, what have we got for breakfast today?" she asked as if to herself. "Pancakes, eggs, and bacon? Not bad," she remarked teasingly. "How is your 'nutritional liquid?' Not too hot or not too cold, I hope," she quipped, mimicking the Goldilocks story. "*Bon appetit!*"

After first mess, which didn't take too long, Lyuba herded them all back to their quarters. "Okay, I'd like to do the formal introductions to Ana a pair at a time. Who's first?" she asked, taking her place at the central table.

"We're ready," announced Gagandeep. "Wan and I'll go first, if that's okay with everyone else." With no one objecting, Gagandeep and Wan joined Lyuba at the table and sat down.

"While we're waiting our turn, I'll go take a shower," said John.

He looked at Xia to see if she wanted to join him, but she replied, "Wan and I already showered earlier before you woke up."

John grabbed his toiletries, a change of coveralls, and headed across the hall to the head. He stripped off all his clothing, depositing them in a large hamper, and then planted himself squarely in front of the mirror. He immediately decided the bald look was not for him, especially not the bald look sans eyebrows. Looking at his naked body barren of any hair at all, he couldn't decide if he looked like an old man or a grotesque, overgrown child. He turned sideways one way and then the other, then patted his stomach. As soon as they got settled in on the planet, he was going to start another exercise program, he promised himself.

John moved to the irradiation booth, put on the small eye shields, raised his arms over his head, and spread his legs. A soft hum indicated that all bacteria, viruses, and any other microbes were being removed from his body. He had just eased into the shower and was adjusting the temperature of the water when Zawadi startled him by slipping in behind him. "Mind if I join you?" she asked as she moved to the other side of the shower stall and turned on the water there.

"No, of course not," John stammered. All the facilities were fully co-ed. It was that way from day one of the training program. No gender distinction was made whatsoever except in assigning partners. It was accepted knowledge that a male/female pair had a significantly better chance of bonding and becoming a successful team than same-gender pairs. To assist in this male/female pairing, all colonists were given medication to lower their sexual drives: Libidebb™, which was patented and distributed by the One World Government. The drug works on both men and women. In men, it increases their level of the hormone prolactin, which, in turn, lowers the level of testosterone. In women, it acts as an aromatase inhibitor that lowers the levels of estrogen. The colonists and crew were rendered disinterested in sexual activities, but not sterile. This would reduce any sexually based stress while living communally in the tight confines of the spaceship. After the colony was set up and established, by stopping the medication, the colonists and crew would be fully functional and capable of carrying on the primary mission: the proliferation of the human species throughout the cosmos.

Disinterested or not, John intentionally kept his back to Zawadi and started lathering up his chest and legs. When fully soaped up, he turned around to face her. She was a very impressive sight! Zawadi stood at least two meters tall, maybe more. John considered himself relatively tall at one-hundred eighty-one centimeters, certainly not short, but she towered over him. Her body was very lean. She had small breasts and was very muscular. She had just a hint of a washboard stomach like all men wanted for themselves. Her skin tone was the darkest he'd ever seen, almost a blue-black. It was not common at all to see someone as dark as this since most people, as John was himself, had a mixture of ethnicities in their ancestry. Her wet, black skin shone brightly in the sharp ceiling light and was a stark contrast from the white, soapy foam smeared here and there along her body. He found himself staring just a little too long, so he quickly pointed and asked, "What's that necklace around your waist?" he blushed a little thinking, *Is it a necklace or a bracelet, or maybe even a "waist-let"?*

Zawadi smiled and stepped forward, taking the pendant hanging from the fine, silver strand around her waist in her hand and moved her pelvis closer to him, "It's a protective medallion," she explained, turning the small, silver pendant over in her hand. John bent over a bit to look more closely but resisted the temptation to reach out and examine it.

"Whose likeness is that on the medallion? Is it you, or

your mother?" John asked nervously.

"No, it's the likeness of a woman who has great honor among my people. She is a woman of great strength and achievements, and the medallion is believed to impart those same qualities to the wearer." John just nodded. "She lived in the late eighteenth and early nineteenth century."

"That long ago?" John exclaimed. "That's about three-hundred-fifty years ago. And you still remember and honor her?" he asked.

"Yes, yes we do," Zawadi responded emphatically. "She led my ancestors out of slavery. Her name was 'Atende,' " she spoke the name reverently.

"Well," said John, "if Atende is supposed to help you be strong, she certainly seems to be doing a very good job, and I think your partner, Malcolm, would definitely agree!" he added with a wink.

"Ha! Malcolm…Yes, Malcolm could be a problem for me if I were not strong. He needs someone strong. I feel it. We need to work together, and I will be strong for both of us." Her straightforwardness surprised him. He just nodded and could at first think of nothing to say. Her eyes ran up and down his body, making him feel a little uncomfortable.

He finally blurted out, "I'm going to start an exercise program as soon as we land."

She then suddenly moved even closer to him and put her soapy hand flat on his chest. "But you," she said slowly and intently while looking him square in the eye, "are strong here," gently patting his chest over his heart. I've seen you with Xia. You're a good man. You have a good heart, and you two seem to make a good team." She took her hand away and slowly backed up to her end of the shower. She stood there in the steaming water, smiling, and looking at him for just a few seconds before she turned, finished rinsing off, and left the shower as quickly as she had come.

John stood in the shower, almost in awe. As he slowly finished rinsing, he thought how lucky he was to have her on the team. He must tell Xia about her.

When John returned to the quarters, Lyuba had finished with Gagandeep and Wan and was now sitting with Zawadi and Malcolm. Gagandeep and Wan were nowhere to be seen. Zawadi looked up from the table and smiled at John as he entered the room. He nodded back at her in acknowledgment.

Xia was sitting on her bunk, so John immediately joined her. "I guess the first computer lesson doesn't take very long," John observed. "Lyuba has moved on to Zawadi and Malcolm already."

"No," Xia replied. "Only about twenty minutes – ship-time, which is about twenty-four minutes Earth-time," she added slyly.

"Ship-time and Earth-time? You must have been practicing," John said, smiling at Xia. "I'm proud of you!" Xia blushed and lowered her head. "No, I really mean it. I know I don't tell you that often enough, but I am very proud of you, and I'm especially proud and happy that we haven't been separated. That we're still on the same team."

Xia blushed even more. "I'm pleased too," was all she replied. "Did you get a chance to talk with Zawadi in the shower?" she added, wanting to change the subject.

"Yes, yes I did."

"And...?" Xia prompted.

"And...she is amazing. She is just as amazing as she looks. And she likes you too," was all that John could say.

"Okay, enough, Malcolm," came a loud retort from

the table. "It's time for me to get John and Xia introduced to Ana," Lyuba continued firmly, hoping to end the endless barrage of Malcolm's questions. Zawadi got up sporting a wry smile and headed back to their bunk area. Wearing a long face, Malcolm followed a couple paces behind.

John and Xia moved to the table, and Zawadi and Malcolm left the room. "I won't say 'Welcome Aboard.' I'm sure you've had enough of that for a while," Lyuba started off. "Today, I'm just going to get you set up with Ana. After that, you should be able to do most anything you want on your own, but if you have any questions Ana can't answer, feel free to ask me. But if Ana can't answer them, I'm pretty sure I won't be able to answer them either.

"Ana is not much different than the Project Sixth Day computers you trained with on Earth. Like them, she is voice-activated and incorporates both voice recognition for security and speech recognition to accept commands or questions. The only significant upgrade to this model is the analog processing. Ana has both a large set of massively parallel, analog processors along with her digital processors. The digital processing runs in the background and is used for all the usual digitized data input, storage, and output, and for all precise mathematical calculations. In the foreground is the analog processing modules which do all the voice and speech recognition, command and question parsing and input, audible response output, quick mathematical approximations, and, most importantly of all, the decision-making activities.

"Why are analog processes better for decision making?" asked John.

"Decision-making algorithms in digital computers all just attempt to emulate analog processes anyway. In a digital system, a bit is either on or off, an answer is either yes or no, right or wrong," replied Lyuba.

"But digital computers didn't always give you a yes or a no. They would give you a qualified yes or no, or give you a probability which you could apply to a decision matrix which also contained risk/reward factors," John countered.

"Yes, but all those processes were applied to give a set of tables in order to emulate an analog curve, just as in order to draw a circle on a digital screen, the individual pixels are arranged in such a way as to emulate a smooth curve. When you zoom in on them, you'll find they are actually more like a staircase." John still did not look convinced, so Lyuba added, "Or you can think of it like the old adage about the mathematician and the artist."

"What adage is that?" John prompted.

Lyuba sat back in her chair and began, "Once there were two men, a mathematician, and an artist. They were led into a room with a beautiful woman standing against the far wall. They were told they could advance towards her halfway, and then continue on half of the remaining distance, and then half of the remaining distance, and then halfway again, and so on. After being told the conditions, the mathematician sat down with a loud sigh, while the artist started quickly stepping towards the woman. The mathematician just laughed and called out mockingly, 'Just what do you think you're doing? If you can only advance halfway, and then half of the remaining distance, and then halfway again, you'll never reach the woman.' To which the artist replied, 'Yeah, I know. But I'll get close enough...' " They all laughed. "The mathematician's approach was digital and exact, whereas the artist's approach was analog and approximate – close enough."

"Are you ready to get started now?" she asked. Both

John and Xia nodded, yes. "Ana, I've got two more new users for you," announced Lyuba to seemingly no one.

"Yes, Lyuba, I'm ready," came the disembodied reply. Ana's voice was pleasant and had a slight English accent. She reminded John of his aunt.

"Ana, these next two users will also be authorized under the category of colonists, but place these two under the sub-category of guardians. Give them all the access, storage, and modification authority defined and specified for that profile, and give them each a separate private area to use as they please."

"Yes, Lyuba," Ana acknowledged. "Please state your ID." Xia looked at John silently asking him to go first.

"My – ID – is – GM – 5," John stated loudly and slowly.

"You don't have to be so loud, or talk so slowly," Lyuba advised. "Just speak normally."

"What is your familiar name?" Ana continued.

"Do you mean what name do I want you to call me?" John asked.

"When you're asking Ana a question, you should address her first. That's not so much of a rule as a good habit to get into, to prevent confusion. Just preface your question with 'Ana.' If you're responding to one of her questions, you don't have to do that," instructed Lyuba.

John tried again, "Ana, do you mean the name I want you to call me?"

"Yes," replied Ana succinctly.

" 'John.' I want you to refer to me as 'John.' "

"John, please tell me a little about yourself."

John looked at Lyuba as if questioning the request, but Lyuba made a hand gesture urging him to respond. "Well, I was born in Area 2 in 2120. I was only told both my egg and sperm donors were predominately Caucasian. Later, DNA testing proved that correct and narrowed one of them down to a part of Area 5 that was historically called Ireland. I attended school at…"

"John, thank you," Ana abruptly interrupted. "That will be sufficient. I've been able to establish your voice profile and speech patterns according to specifications."

John looked offended.

After a slight pause, Ana continued, presumably addressing the second new user, "Please state your ID."

Xia responded, "GF-10."

"What is your familiar name?" Ana continued.

" 'Xiaoli,' I mean 'Xia.' I want you to call me 'Xia.' "

"Xia, please tell me a little about yourself."

"I was born in Area 9 in 2122. My donors were predominately of Chinese ancestry. I never had any DNA testing done."

"Xia, thank you," Ana advised. "That will be sufficient. I detect from your speech patterns that you are not a native English-speaker. Do you want to converse in English or some dialect of Chinese? I am capable of conversing in over four hundred Chinese dialects."

"No, my Chinese-speaking era was a long time ago. I'd prefer interacting with you in English."

"John and Xia, your user profiles are now complete. I look forward to working with you both," Ana concluded. "Lyuba, I am now finished with your request."

Lyuba responded, "Yes, Ana, thanks," and turning to John and Xia, she added, "There's no need to advise Ana you are finished with her. She wouldn't know what that meant. Her work is never finished. She is available for your inquiries every second of every day.

"I've got just a few more things for you. You can access Ana verbally anywhere onboard the ship. If you want a hologram display, they are available at all tables you find onboard, and a few other places also, like the back wall of the mess hall. All you have to do is ask." She then demonstrated," Ana, Project Sixth Day logo display please," and with that, a hologram appeared as if from thin air, which in fact, was not "as if" at all, but that was exactly what it did – appear from thin air. The hologram had the Project Sixth Day logo with the motto below. "You can easily adjust the holographic display," she continued, demonstrating each of the commands, "Ana, zoom in," and the view zoomed-in to a close-up of the logo. "Zoom out," and the entire logo image receded into the distance. "Pan left, pan right. Rotate vertically three-hundred and sixty degrees. Rotate horizontally. Now stop and center. Return to the default view." Ana manipulated the hologram through all the various gymnastic moves and contortions flawlessly.

Then, reaching down, Lyuba brought up two e-tablets. "Through these, you may access Ana anywhere within a one-thousand-kilometer radius, and Ana can transmit both audio replies and holographic displays to you using the e-tablets. You don't need these while onboard, but you'll probably use them after we land and set up the colony," she advised. "You should start learning how to use them now, and the best way to do that is to start working with Ana to completely inventory all the equipment you'll need to perform your functions as guardians. And, of course, check up on the zygotes. They're the reason you're here. Like I told the others, you will be in for some surprises," she warned ominously. "This mission is not exactly the same as the one for which you prepared, but the basics are the same.

"Okay, that's it!" Lyuba said as she stood up, then grinned and added, "That is unless you have any Malcolm-like questions."

John and Xia looked quickly at each other before John

replied, "No, I think we're good to go, at least for now. Thanks a lot."

"Yes, thanks a lot," echoed Xia.

With that, Lyuba exited the room and disappeared down the corridor, leaving John and Xia alone. They both looked at each other and said simultaneously, "Lars and Maria..."

"Yes," John asserted, "and Ai and Mohammed. Let's see if we can find out what happened to our old team. Do you want to do it here or find another room?"

"Let's start here," urged Xia. "We can always move to another room if the others return."

They took hold of each other's hand for luck, and John began, "Ana, please give me the current status of the following colonists: NM-3, NF-12, EM-8, and EF-18."

Ana immediately replied, "The current status of NM-3, EM-8, and EF-18 is deceased. The current status of NF-12 is unknown."

John and Xia looked at each other in shock. Xia started sobbing, and John put his arm around her to comfort her but continued, "Ana, deceased? How? When? Where?"

"Yes, deceased. EM-8 and EF-18 were disintegrated by a laser strike on December 18th, 2148, in Area 1, Sector 6, on the grounds of Project Sixth Day. NM-3 died from complications from being prematurely ejected from his cryo-pod on December 20th, at the same location."

Xia got up and went to her bunk to lie down. The news was too much for her. John helped her to her bunk but returned to the table. "Ana, what about Ai, NF-12? You reported her status as unknown."

"Yes, her current status is unknown."

"Ana, what is the last status you have for her?"

"NF-12 was in cryo-suspension and was loaded aboard Ilithya-3 on June 23, 2149. That is the last individual status

I have for NF-12."

"How about Ilithya-3? What status do you have on her?

"Ilithya-3 launched from the Project Sixth Day's spaceport on June 24, 2149. She successfully completed her slingshot around the Sun and engaged her NLS drive on schedule."

" 'NLS?' What's that?" John asked.

"NLS is the TLA for 'near-light speed,' " Ana responded.

" 'TLA?' What's that?"

" 'TLA' is the TLA for 'three-letter acronym,' " Ana said without a hint of sarcasm.

John shook his head in disgust. "Is that the last status you have?" he continued to dig.

"That is the last status I have that you are authorized to access."

"What? Do you mean there are more status reports after that?" John was confused.

"I'm sorry, John, you are not authorized to access that information," droned Ana.

"How can I get access to find out?"

Ana paused and then replied, "John, do you believe information on the current status of either NF-12 or Ilithya-3 is necessary for you or Xia to perform your duties as guardian?"

"No!" John erupted, "That's not why we asked. I asked because Ai is our friend."

"What is a 'friend'?" Ana asked.

"A friend is someone you care about. Someone close to you. Someone who you'd do anything to find out how they are," John implored, "even if it meant breaking some rules."

"I care about your and Xia's work. I consider you both

'close' to me because you are authorized access. I cannot, however, break the rules for you under any circumstances," Ana reasoned. "So, I'm sorry, John, you are not authorized to access that information," repeated Ana.

John was exasperated and a little angry. "What was Ilithya-3's destination?"

"Ilithya-3's destination was the exoplanet KOI-3010.01."

"What is the exoplanet's distance from Earth?"

"KOI-3010.01 is 1,213.4 light-years from Earth," Ana responded matter-of-factly.

"One thousand light-years from Earth? Has someone gone completely crazy?" John exploded.

Ana replied again in her now starting-to-be-annoying, matter-of-factly manner, "Not 'one thousand light-years,' 1,213.4 light-years."

John again shook his head in disgust. "And you can't give me any more status than that, right?"

"That is correct," confirmed Ana.

John got up and walked heavily over to Xia who was sitting sobbing on her bunk. He sat down beside her and put his arm around her. "Did you hear all that?" he asked softly.

Xia looked at him sadly and nodded her head yes. "I feel lost," she whispered.

"So do I," confided John, "So do I."

It wasn't long until the other two pairs of colonists returned almost at the same time. Gagandeep and Wan were the first to offer a report.

"Well, all I can say is the entire nutritional scheme has been turned upside down," Wan complained. "There are a completely different mix plants onboard than we expected, and there are no animals! Where are we to get our protein?"

"Yes," Gagandeep agreed. "Wan and I are going to have a lot of work to do before we land, and afterward, even more!"

"You think your plans have been reshuffled!" whined Malcolm. "The plans for the colony have been almost doubled in size! And we haven't yet been able to determine if we have all the pre-fabricated materials necessary to construct all the buildings."

"Nonsense!" scolded Zawadi. "Yes, the overall size of the colony's footprint has increased, but there have been no additional types of buildings specified. At first look, the inventory seems adequate. We'll have to go through it all with a fine-tooth comb, but I don't think we're going to find any large inconsistencies.

"How about you two?" Zawadi asked, turning towards John and Xia. "What did you find out about the lab and the zygotes?"

Xia looked guiltily at John, but he responded immediately, "Like you, we found some substantial changes, but so far everything looks reasonable. We'll have to do more research after second mess and probably even into tomorrow." Xia looked at him with surprise but understood.

"Speaking of second mess," said Malcolm, "It's almost 12:00 now. What say we all mosey on down to the mess?"

And with that, they tidied up their areas and two by two headed down the corridor to the second mess and their next helping of…liquid nutrients.

Chapter 4

Discovery

When the group arrived at the mess hall for second mess, they found it empty. They later learned that the times for first mess, second mess, etc., were more like markers or timelines in the day, much like the use of the word "noon" or "midnight." They didn't really mean these were the times everyone met to eat. In fact, all the crew just ate whenever they were hungry. They did use the mess hall for meetings, and every so often would all gather for second or third mess to eat together and then discuss some pressing topic or other item of interest.

The colonists did, however, find their expected six glasses of liquid nutrient waiting for them on the two front tables as usual. Malcolm took a sip and announced that he just couldn't drink another drop of the "vile-tasting swill." He got up from the table and went to the front of the room to the window where he'd seen Lyuba get her food this morning. He stuck his head in and seemed to look around for a few seconds, then they heard him utter some muffled words. He returned carrying a small tray with a plate of some kind of noodle dish. He said it tasted like tuna casserole and was pretty good. He also had a glass of some kind of juice that he described as "just okay," but definitely much better than the liquid nutrient. The rest of the colonists stared lustfully at the plate of noodles but dutifully made do with their liquid protein. In about an hour, Malcolm would have much more to say about his meal.

When they returned to their quarters, they split up into teams to continue their research. Zawadi and Malcolm claimed the table in the quarters, which proved fortunate in the coming hours. Gagandeep and Wan went down the corridor to the left, back towards the mess hall a couple of doors, to the small room they had found and used this morning. John and Xia went out into the corridor and turned right to begin to look for an empty room.

They passed several doors on both sides of the corridor until they finally got to one marked "Observation Room 1-O4." They opened the door and entered. It was a larger room and looked to be the same size as the mess hall. There were molded benches all along three of the walls, and four tables with benches sprouting up from the floor. What made this room special was the fourth wall, the wall opposite the corridor. The whole wall appeared to be a floor-to-ceiling length window. The view was space: a black, star-sprinkled vista that seemed to stretch forever – which it supposedly does. Right in the center of the view was a small, fuzzy, pinkish dot a little larger than the other stars.

"I'll bet that's Kepler-438!" John announced excitedly. "The captain said it was a red dwarf, and that we were no more than a week away." Xia nodded in agreement, and John repeated, "I'll bet that's it."

They both moved to the window to get a closer look. John reached out to touch the reddish star expecting to feel the cold, hard surface of the window. His finger did hit a cold, hard surface, but only after penetrating Kepler-438 about five centimeters.

"Ha!" John exclaimed, "It's only a hologram! It's not a window at all." Xia also reached out and through the projection. "Ana, is this view the view from the spaceship?"

"Yes, John," Ana replied. "It is the view facing the Kepler-438 System."

"Is it life-size? I mean, is that what we'd actually see if we looked at it directly?"

"Yes, John. It is, as you say, 'life-size.' Would you like me to zoom in?"

"Yes, please do. Please zoom in enough so we can see the entire system, and especially Kepler-438b."

"I can zoom in to display part of the system," the hologram changed smoothly bringing Kepler-438 closer and closer until the small, reddish star moved to the extreme left of the view and several bright dots were seen, one about a third of the way from the sun to the middle of the wall and one at the extreme right. Ana then continued, "but I cannot display the entire system on this wall with a resolution sharp enough for you to be able to distinguish all five of the planets. Also, Kepler-438b is behind the star right now, so it is not in this view. Would you like me to simulate a rotation of the view so you can see Kepler-438b?"

"Yes, please," replied John. Both he and Xia stood mesmerized by the display. The view started to rotate, and soon, a small, grayish smudge came into view at about the center of the wall and in between the other two planets.

"Kepler-438b," Ana announced.

"Kepler-438b," both John and Xia repeated in unison and sat down at a table nearest the "window" on benches facing the vista.

They sat for a while in silence until Xia said, "Ana, where are the zygotes?"

Ana replied, "The zygotes are on Level 3."

"Are they all okay?" Xia continued.

"Two zygotes expired in transit," Ana informed.

"Really?" Xia asked rhetorically.

"Really," Ana replied. Ana did not engage in or recognize rhetoric.

"No, I mean that surprises me...somewhat. I guess that's not a big problem," Xia mused out loud. "So, there are eight left then? Eight that are still viable and in the cryo-tubes, right?"

"No, there are five hundred and ten that are viable, and yes, they are all in cryo-tubes," droned Ana.

"Five hundred and ten!" John interjected. "We're referring to human zygotes only, not whatever other animal zygotes we might be carrying for the nutritionists."

"There are no non-human zygotes on board. All five hundred and ten zygotes are human," Ana confirmed.

"Please explain," pleaded Xia. "We were expecting only ten human zygotes."

Ana began her explanation as requested, "The missions for Project Sixth Day Phase I all specified ten human zygotes. The purpose of the Phase I missions was to conduct experiments to determine the viability of establishing long-term colonies on uninhabitable Solar System planets." John and Xia nodded in agreement. "The missions involved in Project Sixth Day Phase II specified five-hundred and twelve human zygotes. The purpose of Phase II missions is to establish permanent colonies on habitable exoplanets."

"You mean Phase I was practice colonization, and Phase II is now for real?" asked Xia.

"Yes, you could phrase it that way if you wish," Ana

conceded.

"So, are there then a corresponding increase in all the equipment and supplies needed to support, grow, and finally bring these zygotes to infancy and adolescence?" Xia asked.

"Yes," Ana succinctly replied, "although it is not intended that you initiate these processes on all zygotes simultaneously. This is intended to be done in phases. Sixteen zygotes in each phase are what is recommended, with a period of one to two years in between phases.

John and Xia looked at each other with surprise, "It sounds like we're going to be very busy for many, many years," John replied.

"Yes," Ana confirmed, "anywhere from thirty-two to forty-eight years plus nine months. That would be sixteen phases, either one or two years apart, and then an additional sixteen years, plus nine months to maturity."

John and Xia huddled together to check the math and finally accepted those figures. Xia then asked, "Ana, are all the equipment to support the full cycle for all the zygotes also in working order and on Level 3?"

"Yes," Ana replied.

John now spoke up, "Are there any different types of equipment or supplies, and are all the procedures the same as in Phase I?"

Ana responded, "Yes, the procedures are all the same as Phase I. The only differences are in the quantities, not the qualities."

Xia turned to John, shrugged her shoulders, and said, "Well then, I think we're done here. Aren't we? I mean, we've learned just about all there is to know about our tasks and how they've been affected by the 'change in plans.' "

"Yes," John agreed, "but I have one more question:

why five-hundred and ten? That seems to me to be an odd number."

"No, five hundred and ten is an even number," Ana corrected.

"I mean 'strange!' I mean, five hundred and ten is a strange number," John snapped back. "Why not five hundred and nine, or five hundred and eleven, or three-hundred and two? Why five hundred and ten? Why that particular number?"

Ana began, "The number of zygotes specified for the mission was five hundred and twelve, not five hundred and ten. Two zygotes expired in transit. The number was five hundred and twelve because that is the number of unique zygotes that can be created from sixteen sets of gamete donors."

"Sixteen sets of gamete donors?" John wailed, "Do you mean sixteen couples? Sixteen male and female couples?"

"Yes."

"But the number of unique zygotes from sixteen couples would only be two hundred and fifty-six, which is sixteen squared," John challenged.

"Yes," countered Ana, "but there are two hundred and fifty-six with XX chromosomes and two hundred and fifty-six with XY chromosomes."

"Two-hundred and fifty-six males and two hundred and fifty-six females!" Xia exclaimed.

"Totaling five hundred and twelve," John added, "Ana, who then were the couples?" John asked hesitatingly.

"The sixteen gamete donors were the sixteen Ministers of the One World Government and their partners," Ana reported, matter-of-factly.

John and Xia looked at each other, letting the significance of that last statement fully sink in. John leaned over close to Xia, "So the ministers decided to populate the universe only with their own progeny," John whispered softly.

"It seems so," replied Xia, "What are we going to do?"

John thought for a while and then replied, "Nothing, I guess. What can we do?"

"We could tell the others, the other colonists," Xia offered. "In fact, we should tell the others. We must tell the others," she reasoned. "They have as much right to know about this as we do."

"That sounds right," replied John heavily, "but let me think it over for a while. Okay?"

"Okay," agreed Xia.

With that, they took a final look at the holographic display of the Kepler-438 System and particularly Kepler-438b, which was to be their new home. They left the room and walked back to their quarters, still in some confusion about the significance of what they'd just found out.

When they entered their quarters, they were greeted with a big grin from Zawadi and a series of pitiful groans from Malcolm. Malcolm was lying on his bunk, one leg hanging down towards the floor as if to give him a head start should he choose to get out of bed, which turned out to be exactly why he was laying like that.

"Oh," he groaned, and then suddenly rolled out of his bunk and headed for the door, "Here come the cramps again!"

Zawadi just smiled and continued working with Ana on some details regarding the changes in the structures specified in the Phase II plans. John and Xia moved to the table and sat down opposite her. After Malcolm had darted across the hall and into the head, she confided that this had started about thirty minutes after they had returned from second mess and has continued ever since.

"I think it's become even worse!" she chuckled. "That will teach him to turn up his nose at the nutritional liquid prescribed for him by the doctor in favor of some 'real' food," she snorted. "Ha!"

John and Xia smiled and chuckled a little themselves. John noticed how Xia's eyes sparkled when she was happy. He hoped to see that more often.

Gagandeep and Wan returned before Malcolm. Zawadi gleefully filled them in on all the details which seemed to tickle Wan somewhat, but Gagandeep just acknowledged Malcolm's condition with a stoic, "I hope he's better soon."

The five of them sat at the table and talked casually about their afternoon. Zawadi reported on her analysis of the Phase II civil engineering requirements, equipment, and systems, but according to her, it was all able to be done. She and Malcolm were going to go up to Level 3 to do a physical inventory tomorrow. Gagandeep and Wan likewise reported that in spite of their first impression, everything they were likely to need should be onboard and on Level 3. They also wanted to do a physical inspection and arranged with Zawadi to go with her and Malcolm in the morning.

When it came time for John and Xia to report, John delivered the news about the five hundred and ten zygotes and the corresponding increase in equipment and supplies. The others were amazed at the number but understood better when Xia explained the differences in the purposes of Phase I and Phase II: practice colonization versus actual colonization, and also the new plan to break the nurturing procedures into phases. Neither John nor Xia, as they had agreed, mentioned anything about the role the ministers played in gamete donation.

During the de-briefing, Malcolm floated in and out of

the meeting, or perhaps it would be better described as unexpectedly and suddenly darted in and out of the meeting. Soon, it was time to go down to third mess.

"Time for third mess," Zawadi taunted. "Malcolm, are you having the nutritional liquid tonight, or are you up for some more exotic fare? Tuna, perhaps?" Malcolm just groaned and indicated he would not be joining the group for mess that night.

The group of five went down the corridor to the mess hall and found their nutritional liquid waiting for them as usual. They drank them down quickly, and all returned to their quarters. Arranging themselves around the table in pairs, sans Malcolm, they talked casually about the other aspects of the voyage until John and Xia described the hologram in Observation Room 1-O4.

"I want to see that!" exclaimed Wan.

"Yes, let's move our chat session down there," suggested Zawadi. They all left, except Malcolm, who, exhausted from his gastrointestinal ordeal, had finally fallen asleep in his bunk.

"Wow!" exclaimed Wan when she entered the observation room and saw the hologram of the Kepler-438 System. "Wow!"

"Yep," agreed Zawadi, "I think 'Wow!' does it for me, too!"

"And Ana can rotate the view around and zoom in or out however you'd like. In fact, Kepler-438b is actually on the other side of the star right now." Everyone was notably impressed.

"Ana," Zawadi began, "zoom in on Kepler-438b." The planet grew larger and larger until it filled the wall. "Ana, it's all gray and fuzzy. Why?" she asked.

"This is the best representation of Kepler-438b I have. In all the views I have stored, none of them show any features of the planet's surface. It may be covered in clouds all of the time. That's my guess," explained Ana.

"Your guess?" chirped John. "You mean you're a computer that makes guesses?"

"I use that term the same way humans do. I mean, I come to an assumption based on incomplete data. That's a function of my analog, analytical-processing programs. Would you rather I revert to the term 'assumption?' "

"No, 'guess' is perfectly fine with me. I guess at things all the time," John admitted. "I have no problem with that."

The five colonists settled in around the tables nearest the hologram and continued their discussions. Occasionally, one of them would command Ana to tweak the hologram, zooming out or rotating the view. After a while, John and Xia excused themselves and moved to a table near the door. They sat close together and spoke quietly enough so the others couldn't hear. Zawadi noticed this and smiled. She assumed by the way they interacted, they were lovers and were sharing intimate secrets. She was right about the "intimate" nature of the secrets.

John and Xia were discussing whether or not to tell the others about the ministers' role in creating the zygotes, and the implication that this entire mission, and maybe the entire Project Sixth Day's purpose, was to ensure the continuation of the ministers' bloodlines. They finally decided they needed to tell the others, but agreed not to try to lead them to any conclusions, like the one they had already made.

Just before they returned to the group table, Malcolm strode in and took a seat beside Zawadi. He was looking much better. After John and Xia were seated again, John began, "Xia and I have one more thing to report. It concerns the specific number of zygotes and their origins."

"Go on," urged Wan.

"There were five-hundred and twelve zygotes because they are all from sixteen pairs of gamete donors," John reported.

"And there were two-hundred and fifty-six males and two hundred and fifty-six females," Xia interrupted and finished his sentence."

"Did you ask who the donors were?" questioned Gagandeep?

"Yes, we did," replied John. "They were the sixteen ministers and their partners."

"The sixteen ministers on the High Council of the One World Government?" Zawadi asked suspiciously.

"Yes," verified Xia.

"I'm not sure that really means anything," Malcolm chimed in. "After all, they were in the middle of changing all their plans, and what with the insurgents and all, where else could they easily acquire the eggs and sperm?" he reasoned. "I'm sure they were under a lot of heavy deadlines."

Gagandeep also spoke up, supporting Malcolm, "Yes, and the sixteen ministers are all from different areas of the Earth. They are as good a mix of ethnicities as you could find in one place. Don't you think?"

"Yes, but it still sounds a little suspicious," admitted Wan, "but what difference does it make? The zygotes are still human, and we're still obligated to treat them with respect and do the best we can for them."

"You're right," agreed Xia, "and that's just the conclusion John and I came to also."

"Besides," Malcolm continued, "we can always make our own zygotes," and with a leer towards Zawadi added, "the old-fashioned way.

"You wish," retorted Zawadi, "Dream on! I think I'm

going to have to tell the doctor to increase your dosage of Libidebb™," she teased.

After an awkward silence, Gagandeep asked, "Are you sure all those five hundred and something zygotes are human? Wan and I searched for some animals in cryo-suspension that we could start farming for protein but came up empty-handed."

"Yes, we're sure," replied John, "but we can check again. Ana, how many zygotes are in cryo?"

"There are five hundred and ten viable zygotes in cryo-suspension," Ana replied.

Gagandeep interrupted, "Ana, how many humans are in cryo-suspension?"

"There are currently five hundred and twelve humans in cryo-suspension."

After an awkward silence, John challenged, "Ana, I thought you said there were five hundred and ten human zygotes in cryo-suspension."

"I did," Ana confirmed, "but there are five-hundred and twelve humans in total in cryo-suspension."

"Then what are the other two?" John asked.

"The other two humans are adults," came Ana's surprising answer.

"Two adults? Who are they?" John queried.

Ana paused a few seconds and then replied, "I'm sorry, John, you are not authorized to access that information."

John looked at the other colonists and then became more insistent, "What are their IDs?"

"I'm sorry, John, you are not authorized to access that information."

"Ana," Zawadi moved to help, "where are these two human adults located?"

"I'm sorry, Zawadi, you are not authorized to access

that information." It appeared they had come to a dead end.

The six colonists all huddled together on one of the benches and discussed the matter. Again, there was no resolution forthcoming, and again, there were suggestions that even this information, although surprising, was not really that alarming or critical. After thirty minutes or so, they rose to return to their quarters. John and Xia were the last to the door. John suddenly grabbed Xia's arm and motioned her to stay. No one else noticed.

After everyone else had departed, John and Xia sat down again at the table. "What John? What do you want?" Xia asked, sounding perplexed.

"I want to try Ana again to find out more about these two mysterious humans in cryo." John sounded determined. "Ana," he began, "who are the two humans still in cryo?"

"I'm sorry, John, you are not authorized to access that information."

"Why not?" John pressed.

"That information is not essential for you to perform your duties."

"When Lyuba instructed you to set up our accounts, she instructed you to give us all the assistance we needed to do our jobs, didn't she?" John continued.

"Yes, John, she did."

"And part of our job as guardians is the responsibility for all humans in cryo, right?" John argued.

"No, John. Guardians have responsibility and complete access to information about the human zygotes in cryo-suspension. Not all humans."

John looked intently at Xia, signaling her to keep quiet and said, "Yes, that was the scope of our responsibilities for Phase I of the project, but in Phase II, we were given responsibilities for <u>all</u> humans in cryo."

"By whom?" asked Ana.

"By the Ministers of the High Council themselves," asserted John forcefully, "and they expect you and everyone else on this mission to fully assist us to fulfill our responsibilities."

There were a couple seconds of silence, and then Ana responded, "That is not included in the description of your responsibilities as defined in my most recent data set."

"Who must I talk with to address this discrepancy and correct the error in our access authorization areas?" John pressed on.

"There is no error. If you'd like to change your access authorization levels, you must talk with Lyuba," Ana informed him. "She is the only one who has the authority to make changes like that."

"Hey, I'm not asking for you to do anything wrong, or something that would jeopardize the mission. I just want to know who the two humans are."

"I'm sorry, John, you are not authorized to access that information."

John sighed, sat back, and decided to try a different tack, "A friend would give me that information."

There were another few seconds of silence. Ana finally responded with a new tone in her voice, a determined tone, "We've discussed this before. Are you asking me to break the rules again? How could that be warranted in this situation?"

John thought for a moment and then said, "A friend is someone who cares more for your needs than their own," his eyes met Xia's. "A friend would help you do whatever you thought was important for you. A friend would help you, even if they had to break the rules."

"I have no needs," Ana responded. "My sole purpose

is to fulfill your needs as they apply to your mission, but I must do that within the rules. I cannot choose the break the rules."

"Yes," John quickly responded and added, "A friend might not break the rules to help themselves, but they would break the rules to help their friend. That's what 'friend' means to humans, and it's one of our most important relationships." John said, all this while his eyes were locked on Xia's.

Ana paused again for a bit and then replied in her usual, matter-of-fact tone, "Then John, I cannot be your friend. I cannot break the rules, not for my sake and not for yours."

"Jeez!" exclaimed John as he rocked back on the bench and then abruptly stood up. He turned to Xia, "Let's go. We're wasting our time here." And with that, he and Xia exited the observation room and returned to their quarters.

When they entered the room, they saw everyone had already turned in for the night – except for Malcolm. He was pacing back and forth and finally sat down at the central table. "Anyone up for a game of chess?" he asked weakly." John and Xia just shook their heads no, and, without any more talk, they readied themselves for bed and climbed into their respective bunks.

John was getting settled in and was just about to fall asleep when Malcolm loudly asked, "Hey? Is there anyone still awake? Who's hungry besides me?"

There was no reply.

Chapter 5

Preparation

Five of the colonists rose early the next morning and were all able to take showers and freshen up before first mess at 06:00. When they were ready to leave, Malcolm was still asleep. Gagandeep expressed some concern and announced he would wait for him, but the other four left and walked down the corridor to the mess hall.

Their first meal that morning could truly be called "breakfast," since they finally were allowed to break their physician-imposed fast of only the liquid nutrient. They still were given glasses of liquid nutrient, however, but this time they were accompanied with oatmeal. They were all very happy.

As they were returning to their quarters, Malcolm and Gagandeep were headed the other way to the mess hall. "What's for breakfast?" Malcolm asked. "Eggs and waffles? Toast with butter and jam?" They all laughed and told him he'd just have to wait and be surprised.

The group began to settle in, and their days became more and more routine. Their main responsibility now and until landing was to acquaint themselves with the changes in their project duties as a result of the new Phase II goals and objectives.

For the nutritionists, Gagandeep and Wan, that meant figuring out how they were going to ensure a self-sustaining food supply for the new colony relying only on the few Earth plants in their inventory, no animals, and a finite supply of synthetic foods, vitamins, minerals, and other fundamental nutrients. These would not last forever. They knew they were going to be very dependent upon locating, testing, and discovering native food sources on Kepler-438b; and then devising a system to domesticate and cultivate them. Experimenting with native flora and fauna as potential food sources was only a very small part of their duties for Phase I. For Phase II, it would be the most important part.

After conducting an extensive inventory of their equipment and supplies, and in order to prepare themselves for their new challenge, Gagandeep and Wan spent most of their days working with Ana to locate and study every digitized textbook and research paper that had any relevance to their tasks. They knew it would be a Herculean effort and one for which they were now unprepared, but one on which the entire success or failure of the mission depended.

The civil engineers, Zawadi and Malcolm, had a lot of changes in plans to figure out how to accommodate also, but their changes were mainly ones of scale, not substance. The plans for the Phase II colony were virtually the same as for the Phase I except there were larger spaces required for the greenhouse, the laboratory where the zygotes would be housed and serviced, and a brand new, large, living area for which there was no real explanation. On the other hand, they no longer had requirements for animal pens, and since Kepler-438b was assumed to be habitable, there would be no, or at least less, need for interior environmental controls. Zawadi and Malcolm spent most of their time pouring over their inventory, matching it to the building plans Ana helped them find, and familiarizing themselves with all of their equipment, which included several new, advanced types of construction robots.

Like the civil engineers, John and Xia, the guardians, also had mainly a Phase I to Phase II scope increase. It was quite an increase. Instead of ten zygotes, they were going to be responsible for five hundred and ten at last count. They were going to have to nurture the zygotes through their entire growth cycle: zygote, embryo, fetus – and then of course birth; and then on through infancy, toddler, and into adolescence. They had all the equipment, such as artificial wombs, they needed to cultivate sixteen zygotes concurrently, and all the nutrients for the planned-for five-hundred and twelve. The timeline would be the most difficult to resolve.

On Earth-time, the basic timeline is zygote to embryo, one week; embryo to fetus, seven weeks; fetus to fully developed baby ready for birth, thirty-two weeks. The whole term totals forty weeks. Calibrating that to Kepler-438b-time is straightforward enough, but there is also the possibility that the entire process might just re-orient itself to Kepler-438b's circadian cycle.

Xia finally came up with the suggestion that they limit their first incubation attempts to a small set of zygotes, perhaps only four. That way, they could daily examine the rapidity of the blastulation, and from the results, project a new timeline, if necessary, for the embryo and fetus development; and from that, project a more exact duration of the entire artificial gestation period.

Xia presented her recommendation to the captain just two days before the scheduled landing. After a short discussion, it was approved.

The mystery of the two humans in cryo-suspension somewhere on the ship continued to eat away at John. Every time he and Xia would go to Level 3 to inspect the zygotes in cryo-suspension or some of the equipment, he would snoop around the entire level, searching for the two cryo-pods housing the unknown humans. He looked through all the paperwork that was all filed near the zygotes' cryo-pods. There wasn't much of that, anyway, since all the important information was stored digitally. He even had jimmied his way into several locked drawers in spite of a scolding Ana, all to no avail. After four days and many hours spent on Level 3, at least twenty-five percent of which John had dedicated to his searching, the only real leads he had found were three locked doors. Ana, of course, would not open those doors for him, and frankly, John was getting tired of hearing Ana's repetitive, monotonous "I'm sorry, John, you are not authorized..." responses.

The six colonists had developed a routine of getting together after third mess in the observation room to discuss their day's activities and share information. They also enjoyed viewing the ever-nearing Kepler-438 System from the perspective of the spaceship. Over the past four days, Kepler-438b had emerged from behind the small, reddish star, and the ship seemed to be slowly swooping in towards it. One of their favorite requests of Ana was to back up the hologram to a week ago, and then fast forward to the present, and, of course, then continue projecting forward in time until orbit around Kepler-438b was simulated. The biggest disappointment was the lack of details available on the planet itself. The only representation Ana could provide was still just a fuzzy, gray ball, although Ana was able to now definitely confirm that the gray fuzz was a result of a seemingly planet-wide cloud cover.

It was during one of these discussions that John got a useful clue. Zawadi and Malcolm were arguing, as usual, about a multi-room area that was an addition to the plans for the colony in Phase II. The unit would occupy the entire third floor of the main, domed structure where all the public resources were scheduled to be located. Zawadi thought the multi-room area was meant to be used for meeting rooms. There would be one, very large room for large meetings, three conference rooms, one large and two medium-sized, a kitchen, a large outdoor deck area, and a couple washrooms. One strange thing with the design was one of the washrooms was only accessible from the large conference room.

Malcolm argued that the area was going to be living quarters. What Zawadi called the large, central meeting area was the living area, the conference rooms were bedrooms or studies, the largest, with the washroom, being the "master" bedroom suite. He suggested that it was going to be occupied by the flight crew.

Zawadi countered that the regular domiciles already had units specified for all four of the flight crew's IDs, and if they were to be domiciled in this new area, two of them would have to share the "master" bedroom.

"So?" interrupted Malcolm, "Don't you think the captain and the first officer might be shacking-up?"

"Maybe," conceded Zawadi, "but what about their regular units? Why would Plan II provide a whole new area for the crew but still have their Plan I units?"

Malcolm shrugged that argument off with, "Who knows? Maybe it's just an oversight. Maybe they didn't have time to re-assign those units and were going to leave that up to us," he offered, "Who cares?"

"Okay," continued Zawadi, "maybe it was an oversight, but why would they label the area MM-2 and MF-2? Wouldn't you assume the 'M' classification stands for 'meeting?' "

A light started to glow dimly in John's mind, "Did you ask Ana about this?"

"No," replied Zawadi and Malcolm in unison.

"Well then, let's try," suggested John, "Ana, what does the top-level ID classification 'M' stand for?"

"I'm sorry, John, you are not authorized to access that information," Ana droned out.

The group was stunned, all but John, "Ana, what does the top-level ID classification 'A' stand for?"

"There is no top-level ID classification 'A,'" Ana replied.

John probed again, "Ana, what does the top-level ID classification 'Q' stand for?"

"There is no top-level ID classification 'Q,'" Ana replied.

"And now for the coup-de-grâce," whispered John to the group, "Ana, what does the top-level ID classification 'M' stand for?"

"I'm sorry, John, you are not authorized to access that information," Ana replied again.

The six colonists all leaned back from their tables a little and silently looked around at each other. They all realized what had just happened. John had turned Ana's non-answer into an answer of sorts.

"So, we know that 'M' is a valid, top-level ID classification, but we don't know what it means," explained John, "I think these IDs belong to the two humans in cryo."

The six colonists put that topic aside and continued to share other information they had discovered that day and continue bonding as a group.

At 22:00, they decided to call it a night and head back to their quarters. Upon arriving, there they found the doctor waiting for them.

"Good evening. Ana told me you had been down in the observation room and were heading back here. I've got a couple things to discuss with you," he said with a serious tone. "Please, all of you, take a seat," he prompted, motioning toward the central table. When they were all settled in, he remained standing and continued while circling them at a slow gait, "Ana has told me several of you have been repeatedly requesting information for which you are not authorized." The group shifted nervously in their seats. "Why is this?"

Everyone looked at John and continued to do so until he spoke up, "That's my question too," John retorted defiantly. "Why are some of our requests for information being denied?"

The doctor didn't receive this challenge very well. He glared at John, then softened a bit and asked, "What have you been asking, and why?"

"We found out some things that are disturbing," John finally replied.

The doctor now zeroed-in on this and continued his interrogation, "What kind of information did you find out?"

"We discovered that there were two additional humans on board still in cryo," John immediately admitted. He decided he wouldn't bring up the issue about the ministerial donors for all the five hundred plus zygotes. "Xia and I found that out while running our inventory on the zygotes."

"What else do you know," the doctor probed and added, "or think you know."

"We think we know their IDs," John offered.

"You do? How did you come by these?" the doctor asked suspiciously.

"Zawadi and Malcolm told us about the Phase II plans for a new, multi-room area on the top floor of the central building. They thought it was either a big meeting area or perhaps even a domicile. The plans themselves and some of the rooms had what looked like IDs on them."

"What were the markings that looked like IDs?"

"They were 'M' something," stammered John.

"The overall plan was labeled MM-2, and MF-2 was also noted," Zawadi filled in.

The doctor paused for a moment and then remarked, "And you thought these were human IDs?"

"Yes," John confirmed, "but Ana wouldn't tell us what the top-level 'M' classification meant."

"Well, I can confirm there are indeed two humans on board still in cryo-suspension," the doctor revealed, "but I can't confirm those are their IDs or even if they are human IDs. I can tell you these two will be kept in cryo-suspension until after we land, but then they will be revived. You'll all meet them, and they will live freely among us as part of the colony."

"Who are they?" Malcolm demanded.

"All in due time, all in due time," the doctor chided, "Who they are and why they are here have absolutely no bearing on your duties. As far as I'm concerned, this topic is closed, and I suggest you keep it that way," the doctor scowled as he looked around the room and especially at John, "And don't continue interrogating Ana for clues. She has a lot more important things to do with her processing cycles now until landing than play Dr. Watson to your Sherlock Holmes' detective work.

Everyone was quiet, and the doctor let the silence

hang over the group for an uncomfortable amount of time. "I now have some important details to tell you about tomorrow's activities," he finally said brusquely. The colonists shifted a little at the table, "As you all know, our landing on Kepler-438b is scheduled for two days from now. There's not a lot you all have to do to prepare for the landing itself, but we do need to show you the Landing Room you'll be asked to report to during the landing, for your safety, of course," he added.

"I'll meet you all in the mess hall at first mess and then escort you to the Landing Room, which is clear to the rear of Level 3. We can then go over the procedures and stage a run-through – show you the room and facilities, assign you all seats, and instruct you on how to use the shoulder harnesses. This was all part of your Phase I training, but we should go over it at least this one last time. It shouldn't take more than an hour."

"Are there any things we need to bring with us for this 'run-through'?" Malcolm asked.

"No, just yourselves – and a good balance. Level 3 has only .3 EG," the doctor advised, "And enough of this snooping! Captain's orders!" With that, he turned and left the room.

* * * *

Long before and ever since the colonists had been awakened from their cryo-suspension, Ana and the flight crew had been preparing for the landing on Kepler-438b. All of the procedures had already been set, had been practiced again and again during training, and also periodically during the flight itself. Radiation readings, exhaustive refractive measurements, and spectral analysis had adequately determined the temperature range and gaseous mixture of Kepler-428b's atmosphere, all confirming human habitability. The only real uncertainty now was the condition and topology of the surface of the planet.

Ilithya-2, having traveled over four-hundred and seventy light-years, had finally achieved orbit around Kepler-438b. Upon arrival, Ana first maneuvered Ilithya-2 into a polar orbit and adjusted the spaceship's relative velocity so its orbit would be one sidereal day. This would enable Ilithya-2 to pass over the planet's equator at different longitudes on each orbit allowing Ana to scan the planet with cloud-penetrating sonar and other technologies to develop a complete map of the planet's surface in eight passes. During this time, all the other preparations for landing were being made by both the ship's crew and the colonists.

The captain and the first officer virtually lived on the bridge during this time. They had bunks there where they could sleep, but sleep did not come easily at this stage of the mission. Most of their attention was centered on the holographic image of the planet's surface Ana was creating in real-time as she scanned. She projected that in a hologram in the meeting room off the bridge. Before the first orbit was even completed, the captain and the first officer thought something was wrong.

"Ana," ordered the captain, "please check the calibrations and returns of your scanning equipment. All we're seeing here is a flat, reddish surface. There doesn't seem to be any topological variation at all."

"All my scanning equipment is working properly, and the holographic projection is correct," Ana reassured and went on to add, "The color is a light red, but the topology is not completely flat. There are some small variations, but none I've encountered so far that exceed .01% variance in the average surface plane. I think you would refer to them as 'rolling hills.'

"There are two other items of interest, though, that you will not detect viewing the hologram," Ana offered voluntarily.

"What are they?" the captain and the first officer asked simultaneously.

"The surface of the planet is showing a couple of other unexpected conditions. Of course, I don't know if these will prove to be global characteristics, but if they do, they will be significant."

"What are they?" the captain repeated.

Ana began slowly, in her school-teacher tone, "The Brinell Hardness Number, BHN, calculated for the surface of Kepler-438b, is considerably less the average for that of the surface of the Earth. Also, the BHNs from different parts of the Earth have quite a variance – from hard granite to soft sand, to water – whereas the individual BHNs I've calculated for the areas scanned so far on Kepler-438b are virtually identical." Ana overlaid the formula for BHNs on Kepler-438b's dissolving hologram.

The captain and the first officer looked at each other and just shrugged their shoulders. "Ana, could you dumb that down a little for us please," requested the first officer.

"Please define 'dumb down,' " requested Ana.

"Summarize," interjected the captain while rolling her eyes.

"That means," replied Ana, "that so far, the surface of Kepler-438b is not only fairly flat but has a uniform hardness, and that hardness has about the equivalency of packing foam."

BHN Force Diagram and Formula

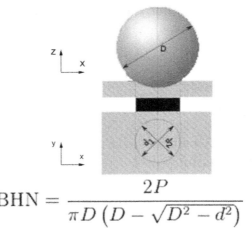

$$\text{BHN} = \frac{2P}{\pi D \left(D - \sqrt{D^2 - d^2} \right)}$$

where:
P = applied force (kgf)
D = diameter of indenter (mm)
d = diameter of indentation (mm)

"Packing foam?" wailed the first officer, "You mean the kind of foam we use to pack the equipment into crates to protect and cushion it?"

"Yes," confirmed Ana.

"Would that support the weight of the ship?" the captain asked anxiously, "and how about a human? Could a human walk on it?" she added nervously.

"Yes, on both counts," Ana replied reassuringly, "The ship can be configured to land on almost any surface, including water. A human, depending on their weight and surface area of their footgear, would depress the surface no more than five centimeters, on average. Also, this sample is less than five percent of the entire surface of the planet. I will have a more complete model in a few days," Ana reminded, "I expect some larger variances."

"Ana's right, we need to wait to see more. No need to get too worried right now," agreed the first officer.

"There is one other thing," Ana reminded.

"Oh, yes, you said there were two unusual things. What is it?" asked the captain.

"The nature of the surface is not inorganic," replied Ana.

"What? Do you mean it is soil that contains a lot of organic material, like loam?" asked the first officer.

"No," replied Ana, "it is a living organism."

"A plant? You mean the entire surface is covered with a plant?" the captain stuttered out.

"No, not a plant, and not an animal – something in between."

This statement was met with complete silence. "Are you sure?" asked the captain when she had gathered her wits and was able to form a question.

"Yes," confirmed Ana, "very sure. I am cross-checking all my remotely stored files to see if I can find any known organism that has similar characteristics, but so far, I have found nothing that even comes close. There are organisms on Earth that do straddle the line between plant and animal, but no life form anywhere near as complex as this one."

The captain and the first officer decided to leave it at that for now, but continually exchanged ideas on some possible, alternate ways to better investigate the planet's surface, and especially any candidate landing sites. They both agreed, however, that for now, they would keep this new, more detailed information about the planet's surface to themselves. Ana was instructed accordingly.

The doctor and the cyberneticist were fully briefed. The doctor was sent down to advise the colonists that the planet's surface details were in the process of being scanned and mapped, but the results would not be available for a couple more days. The colonists' suspicions were immediately aroused. They had already developed a distrust of anything the doctor told them. Lyuba was instructed to re-program Ana to confirm this if asked, but she informed the captain that was impossible. "The best Ana can do is treat the information as restricted, but she cannot tell them an untruth," was Lyuba's bottom line.

As the doctor's "couple more days" turned into three and then four days, the colonists did try to access this information but were dutifully informed by Ana that they were, "...not authorized to access..." Tempers were starting to flare. This rejection of their queries on top of the refusal to divulge the identity of the two unknown humans still in cryo-suspension was beginning to foment unrest. The captain, who had been monitoring their discussions via Ana, finally decided it was time to share the new details on Kepler-438b's surface with them. She called a meeting to be held in the mess hall after third mess on the sixth day of Ana's eight-day scan.

The colonists were all there early, except for Malcolm. The rest of them had already eaten and cleared up their table. The captain and all the rest of the flight crew had arrived and taken their seats at tables at the back of the room. Only the captain, the first officer, and the doctor were fully informed on all the details of Ana's scans up to now. Lyuba and Hoke, the flight engineer, had some briefings over the past several days, but they knew only a little more than the colonists – which was next to nothing. After the colonists had cleared their table, the captain and the flight officer stood up at the back of the room and seemed to be going over a few details in hushed voices when Malcolm finally strolled in, went to the window on the back wall, got his tray of food, and sat down at the front tables. He started eating and then realized everyone was staring at him, "What?" he said defensively, and then resumed eating.

The first officer finally took his place on one of the benches. The captain faced the group assembled and began, "Greetings. It's good to see all of us assembled in one room. We'll have to do this more often," she began, "and after we land in just a few more days, I'm sure we will.

"I've asked you all to come today to bring you up to date on the scan Ana's been conducting on the surface of Kepler-438b, our new home. I think the best thing to do is just to jump right in and show you what Ana's found out, discuss some of the ramifications of that, and then let you know our plans going forward from now until landing."

There being no remarks from the group, she continued, "First of all, be advised that Ana's scans are only eighty percent complete, but because of the speed of our polar orbit and the rotation of the planet, Ana's scanning has reached a good representation of all areas. Ana, please display the hologram of your scanning of Kepler-438b, starting with day-one and continuing until today, and accelerate the timeframe so your six-day scans will be displayed within one minute.

Ana proceeded to do that. The hologram showed Kepler-438b with two small polar areas and eight wedge-shaped areas. The polar area filled in first indicating it had been scanned, and then six of the eight wedge-shaped areas filled in on-by-one indicating Ana's scanning activities. There were only two areas left unscanned when the hologram was brought completely up to date.

Kepler-438b Scanning Sequence and Status

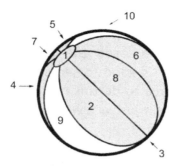

"I don't see any detail," observed Malcolm in between bites of a synthetic pork chop.

"Yes, there isn't much detail," admitted the captain. "Firstly, because of the limitations of the scanning technologies, and secondly, because, frankly, there just isn't much detail."

"What do you mean by that?" Malcolm said, almost as if wondering out loud.

"So far, Ana has found virtually no topological variances. Using terms we are familiar with on Earth, that means there are no mountains or canyons that rise above or sink below the general landscape. The small variances that have been found are more like very gently rolling hills, or even the surface of a lake on a moderately windy day, or the windswept expanse of a large sand desert," explained the captain."

"Is the surface all the same?" asked Wan.

The captain responded, "So far, yes, it does seem to be."

"What is it? Is it all a reddish color like is shown in the hologram?" Gagandeep followed up.

"We don't know for sure," admitted the captain, "and

yes, it is a light red. Ana tells us it's not hard, somewhat soft, but not so soft you can't walk on it. Ana also says it's organic. Our working theory right now is it's some kind of groundcover, like grass or moss."

"Is there water? Gagandeep asked, "We've got to have water to live there. I don't see any bodies of water or rivers."

"Yes, Ana's confirmed the atmosphere is heavy with water vapor. We think any standing water might be covered by this reddish growth," replied the captain, "and there should indeed be liquid water because Ana has also discovered the planet's global, ambient temperature ranges from 28°C to 40°C. In other words, Kepler-438b is warm and humid."

"Perfect for growing crops," Wan happily added.

"How thick is this surface groundcover?" Malcolm chimed in, "Could it interfere with our buildings, especially the foundations?"

The captain shot a nervous glance at the first officer and replied, "We don't know for sure. Ana has not been able to determine that just yet. She has reported that the hardness measurement increases with depth, but did not reach any definite conclusion," After another glance at the first officer she added, "Right now, we are estimating as much as one meter, but it could be more."

Zawadi, who had been silent up until now, finally joined the discussion, "What are your plans going forward?"

The captain looked at the first officer. He rose and moved over to stand beside her to take over the rest of the briefing, "Ana will finish her scan, of course, but assuming she doesn't find any anomalies, we'll have her crunch through all the data and recommend optimal sites for the colony."

"If all the surface is the same, what makes a difference?" challenged Malcolm.

"There's actually not a lot," admitted the first officer, but there are some items to consider. Ana has discovered some things previously unknown before because of Kepler-438b's global cloud cover. Her axial tilt is only 7.8°. Earth's is 23.4°. That means the angle of the light coming from Keplar-438 does not fluctuate across the latitudes as much as does the sunlight on Earth. Simply put, there are only very mild 'seasons' on Kepler-438b. Also, since Kepler-438b's orbital periods are just a little over thirty-five Earth-days, what 'seasons' do occur cycle in just a little over an Earth-month instead of an Earth-year.

"There are some minor variations in humidity and sunlight that filters through the global cloud cover. These might be all variable and not really matter, but we'll ask Ana to crunch the numbers and give us some recommendations," he paused slightly, allowing his eyes to scan the entire assembly, "After all, we only have one shot at this. Ilithya-2 was made to depart Earth, travel to this exoplanet, land, and establish a colony here. She cannot return to orbit and certainly not to Earth – or go somewhere else if this doesn't work out."

This last remark reminded the crew and colonists of the seriousness of their mission. It was nothing they hadn't heard before, and nothing they didn't already know and to which they had unequivocally committed, but being reminded of it here and now caused a shiver to go up their spines and a cold, empty feeling in the pit of their stomachs. There was no turning back. This Kepler-438b was to be their new home.

* * * *

Ana finished her scans on schedule a few days later.

Nothing new was discovered. She then started on the task of comparing all the data and recommending optimal landing sites to the captain and first officer. Because all the data was so similar, that didn't take long at all. In the end, she suggested only two sites which were very close together.

The captain assembled the first officer and the doctor in the meeting room on the bridge. "Ana, please display the two proposed landing sites," the captain commanded.

Kepler-438b Proposed Landing Sites

The first officer immediately asked the most obvious question, "Ana, why only two?"

Ana answered, "There are only two because although there were some assumed, but not validated, disadvantages of locations other than these, there were none that presented calculable advantages."

"Why then these two?" the first officer continued his interrogation.

"The first site represents a site on the equator. Its

coordinates are Latitude North 0°, Longitude West 0°, which would provide for the same angle of sunlight during one orbital cycle. I remind you that cycle is 35.23310 Earth-days or 29.24692 Kepler-439b-days", Ana continued, "The other site is Latitude North 15°, Longitude West 0° which would provide for a slight variation in the angle of sunlight during the full orbital cycle without subjecting the colony to any temperature extremes. For the colonists on board, it would be somewhat reminiscent of the 'seasons' on Earth. This could be fifteen degrees north or south of the equator, it doesn't matter," she added.

"I understand how you calculated the latitudes for the sites since the equator is by definition latitude 0°, but how did you calculate the longitude for the sites?" asked the first officer.

"I didn't calculate the longitude, I assigned it," replied Ana. "Longitude is calculated east or west from an arbitrarily designated line which stretches pole to pole and is given the longitude of zero degrees. Historically on Earth, zero degrees had been assigned to a longitude that intersects the ancient city of Greenwich in a land that used to be called England. My references all confirm this explanation, although some references claim the location itself was just a myth."

"So, we can assign any longitude we want as longitude zero!" remarked the flight engineer with a laugh, "Why not?" The captain and the doctor smiled approvingly.

"How about "north" and "south"? Did you also assign them arbitrarily?" questioned caption.

"No, the planet does have a weak electromagnetic field," Ana explained, "so I assigned the negative pole as "north," as is done on Earth. And although you didn't ask, since Kepler-438b revolves around Kepler-438 in the opposite direction as does Earth, it also rotates in the opposite direction. Because of this, I've assigned the directions of "east" and "west" as opposite also." There was an audible gasp from the crew. "Doing this will, however, maintain the familiar phenomena of the sun "rising" in the east and "setting" in the west, as it is quaintly described in your languages."

After some humorous banter among the crew concerning Ana's last remark, the doctor was the first to express a preference on the location of the sites, "I think, unless some other data comes in, we should seriously consider Site 2 at Latitude North 15°. I recommend that for the very reason, Ana chose it as one of the options – a little variation for the colonists. I think that would be good for their psyche."

"I agree," said the captain, and the first officer nodded his consent.

* * * *

Ana was instructed to maneuver Ilithya-2 out of her current polar orbit and reposition her to a geostationary orbit over the proposed Landing Site 2. Since Landing Site 2 was not on the equator, Ana would have to continually maneuver the ship along the path of an analemma which resembles an asymmetrical figure-eight and is dependent upon four factors: 1) the angle on the planet from which the analemma is viewed which is determined by longitude, or in this case, the viewing angle from the orbiting body to Landing Site 2; 2) the planet's axial tilt; 3) its orbital eccentricity or the amount that its orbit varies from a perfect circle; and 4) the apse line which is also a measurement of the orbital eccentricity. In the case of Kepler-438b and Landing Site 2, only the axial tilt was really relevant due to the short time Ilithya-2 would be holding there. It was from that position, 35,786 km above the surface at a speed of 3.1 km/sec, that Ana would do a more detailed analysis of the proposed landing site, pick exact coordinates, run through the checklists, and reconfigure the ship for landing.

During this time, the colonists and the other two members of the ship's crew were brought together and informed of Ana's landing site recommendations and the captain's decision. There was only a short discussion. Malcolm had to be convinced, of course, but in the end, there was unanimous approval of the selection of Landing Site 2.

Everyone was tasked with preparing the interior of the ship for landing. The landing would be essentially vertical as viewed from both the ship and the planet's surface since Ilithya-2 was now in a geostationary orbit. Ana had to coordinate a slow decrease in Ilithya-2's velocity, taking into consideration several factors. Among these were maintaining a comfortable rate of descent that would stress neither the ship, its passengers, nor its cargo. Another was maintaining vertical-positional integrity above Landing Site 2. The challenge was doing so while balancing such factors as the specific orbital energy, kinetic energy, and potential energy to coordinate a smooth transition of the current orbital altitude of 35,786 km and an orbital speed of 3.1 km/sec to an altitude of zero and an apparent speed also of zero to accomplish the landing at Landing Site 2.

After achieving geostationary orbit, Ana's more intensive scans of Landing Site 2 revealed nothing of note. In the meantime, the crew had accomplished all of their preparations for landing, so the captain set the date and time. Ana would begin Ilithya-2's descent at 08:00 the next day. Ana estimated the descent would take approximately two hours depending on the turbulence encountered when descending through Kepler-438b's thick cloud cover, and any significant surface winds, neither of which had been detected on any of the previous scans.

That evening, the colonists all met in the observation room for what they thought would be their last time. The image of a gray, cloud-covered Kepler-438b filled the hologram on the outside wall. The short evening was filled with only small talk. No one wanted to get into any heavy discussions. Even Malcolm was substantially subdued. They would sleep tonight, rise around 05:00, shower, and take first mess at 06:00. At 07:30, they would assemble in the secure Landing Room. This was a large room with seats and shoulder harnesses. It was located at the opposite end of the ship than the bridge, but on the same level, Level 3. The reason for that, they were told during training, was to maximize the chances of survivability of at least some of the passengers should the ship break up on landing. This design was efficient and necessary, they all supposed but didn't help to bolster their confidence.

Around 22:00, the group began to disperse, couple by couple, and return to their quarters. John and Xia stayed for a while, just sitting in silence and gazing at the hologram of Kepler-438b. This was to be their new home. Many thoughts swirled around in their heads, but they kept them to themselves. They were the last to leave, and when they got to their bunks, everyone else had retired for the night.

John was asleep as soon as his head hit the pillow.

Chapter 6

Landing

*T*his *evening, the jungle had a mysterious air about it. John no longer felt completely at ease. He sat, as usual, on the bank next to the stream, but nothing seemed quite right. The stream gurgled at his feet, but the sound was not soothing. The enveloping canopy which usually gave him a feeling of comfort now looked strange and foreboding.*

Suddenly, he began to rock back and forth involuntarily, like the ground was shaking. Just as he reached out his arms to steady himself, the jungle started dissolving...

"John," called Xia as she gently shook him to arouse him from his sleep, "it's just past 05:00, and time to get up," she coaxed. "Today's the day we land. Today's the day we're going home."

John and Xia showered and dressed. They carefully stored all their gear in their lockers and made sure no loose articles were lying around their area. Even though the landing was supposed to be pretty smooth, everyone did the same just as a precaution.

Just before 06:00, the colonists headed down to the

mess hall. They gathered there together and ate, engaging in small talk. Before they left the mess hall, they each collected several containers of drinking water. They would not be able to return to the mess hall until Ilithya-2 had landed.

They milled around in their quarters for a while, and then all decided to go down to the observation room and wait there as a group for the call for them to assemble in the theater-like Landing Room. At 07:30, the doctor opened the door.

"Ana told me you were all in here," he remarked. "Are you ready to go?" Couple by couple, they followed him down the corridor, up two decks, and down the corridor again to the Landing Room at the rear of Level 3. They carefully shuffled to their assigned seats in the .3 EG, stowed their personal items in the consoles beside them, and strapped themselves in. There was no need for instructions. They had practiced for this moment during their training and here again on the ship. At 07:55, the large hologram-projection area in the front of the room flickered to life, displaying the images of the captain and the first officer.

"Everything is ready," advised the captain. "The crew is all set, the doctor tells me you are all set, and Ana is prepared to start our descent precisely at 08:00. You won't feel anything initially. You may hear some unusual sounds, but we shouldn't hit any turbulence for the first two-thirds of the descent, until about 09:20, and we may not even encounter any then. We should be on the ground by 10:00. After that, you will be instructed to return to your quarters for the rest of the day, although you may take your meals in the mess hall as usual and spend time in the observation area you seem to like to frequent. If all goes well and everything checks out, we should be able to start making exploratory expeditions out and onto the planet's surface tomorrow morning.

"During this descent, Ana will project a view of Kepler-438b and the landing site as it would be seen from the ship. Please feel free to ask her any questions at any time. She's powered by two large arrays of massively-parallel processors, both digital and analog."

"That means she can walk and chew gum at the same time," quipped the doctor.

"The time has now come," the captain announced. "If you are the type that prays, or want to cross your fingers for luck, do it now. Otherwise, just sit back and enjoy Ana's handiwork." Then, the captain commanded, "Ana, begin the descent to Kepler-438b, Landing Site 2."

"Beginning descent," Ana confirmed.

The captain switched off the intercom to the Landing Room and commanded, "Ana, be sure the holographic display available in the Landing Room is gradually retarded until it is displayed with a five-minute lag." She turned to the first officer explaining, "If there are any problems, I want some time to deal with them before those in the Landing Room go into a panic."

Ana began the controlled, virtually vertical, descent by firing thrusters, which pitched Ilithya-2 downward ten degrees while slowly reducing her speed in a carefully calculated ratio to her position over Landing Site 2 and her altitude and speed relative to the rotation of Kepler-438b. At the same time, Ana began the slow cessation of the horizontal rotation of the outer hull that contained Levels 1, 2, and 3; and the coordinated vertical rotation of the individual levels, which would result in a complete 90° repositioning. This was done so the outer walls, which served as the floor while "down" was determined by centrifugal force during flight, to "down" as determined by the full influence of Kepler-438b's gravity field. The occupants felt none of this.

As the descent proceeded, Ana continued to display the "heads-up" view from the front, soon to be the bottom of the spaceship. For the first hour, there was not much to see, just closer and closer views of the planet's global cloud cover. There were, however, some observations that could be made. The first was that the cloud cover was very even, and all virtually the same shade of dull gray. There were no obvious clusters of thicker, dark clouds or sparser, light clouds. The second observation was that there was no evidence of any swirling in the clouds. They seemed to be not only evenly colored but virtually static. This observation was confirmed when finally, at 09:18, Iliytha-2 began descending through the cloud cover itself. This part of the descent lasted for under five minutes. The cloud cover was, as Ana had predicted, relatively shallow, although the clouds themselves were fairly dense and full of water vapor. They contained no turbulence, however, and the descent through the cloud cover was uneventful.

As Iliytha-2 started to break through the bottom of the clouds, there was a chorus of audible gasps from those assembled in the Landing Room. The captain and the first officer on the flight deck, although knowing what to expect and viewing this site five minutes before those in the Landing Room, had also been mesmerized by the first view of Kepler-438b's surface.

It was red. The entire surface of the planet from horizon to horizon was red. There were patches of lighter and darker reds here and there, but no colors other than the red of the surface and the dull gray of the skies were visible. The red surface, as Ana had predicted, was virtually flat with only some very subtle, small, rolling "hills." The total effect was similar to that of seeing an ocean or large body of water in relatively calm conditions. As Ilithya-2 drew nearer and nearer the surface and the anticipation of anything unexpected lessened, the captain notified Ana to catch up her holographic display in the Landing Room to real-time.

It wasn't until close to landing that the hologram provided enough detail to determine that the surface was not just a smooth, solid surface. At first, it just looked like there was some texture to it, and finally, just before the actual landing, the texture was seen to be made up of individual leaves or sprouts, much like that making up Earth moss, but larger – and of course, red. But even with that, the general impression of Kepler-438b was just a static sea of red kelp.

Ilithya-2 set softly down on Kepler-438b. The ship initially tilted slightly to one side, but Ana corrected that by extending the corresponding landing struts. Shortly after the ship attained a level attitude and remained there for a few minutes, the captain's voice came through loud and clear from the bridge to the Landing Room, "Ladies and gentlemen, welcome to Kepler-438b."

The entire Landing Room erupted in cheers. Everyone unharnessed themselves, bounded out of their seats, somewhat carefully though in the .3 EG, and circulated around the room hugging their fellow colonists. They were now home.

The gravity on Kepler-438b was, as expected and simulated on Level 1 during the flight, .9 EG. They were all well used to it now and easily and quickly made their way from the Landing Room on Level 3 through Level 2 to their quarters on Level 1. The levels now were not stacked on top of each other, but, thanks to Ana's synchronized rotation, were positioned side-by-side.

The colonists didn't spend much time in their quarters. They only briefly assembled there and then left en masse for the observation room. It was there they stayed chatting excitedly and commanding Ana to pan in and out, up and down, over and across, to view as much of Kepler-438b's surface as was possible. They only left to take second and third mess in the mess hall, but returned quickly to continue their group and private discussions, or to just sit and gaze out at the landscape. The liveliest discussions were between the guardians and the civil engineers. The guardians already had a number of suggestions for outdoor structures not included in the original plans. They claimed they would need these to assure the new toddlers and adolescents had places to play and congregate. The civil engineers took some notes but promised nothing.

The most popular hologram was Ana's projection of Kepler-438b's groundcover.

Kepler-438b Groundcover

About 22:00, the first officer came in to tell them it was time to retire. "Tomorrow," he teased them, "will be the busiest and most exciting day of your lives." They returned to their quarters and went to bed, but not many of them slept.

By 05:30, they had all arisen, showered, and were sitting in their quarters around the central table counting down the minutes until it was time to go down to the mess hall for first mess. Upon entering the mess hall, they saw all the crew was already there. Everyone greeted them. They got their breakfasts and settled into their tables.

As they were finishing their meals, the captain got up and addressed them all, "Again, welcome to your, I mean our, new home! Last night, while you were sleeping, Ana ran through all her analysis of the atmosphere, temperature, radiation levels, and everything pertinent to assuring your safety on the surface of the planet. All factors tested out as expected, well within acceptable parameters and suitable for human habitation. You'll all be able to leave the ship today and venture out onto the planet's surface for a short period." This brought excited murmurs of approval from the colonists.

"First out will be Zawadi and Malcolm, the civil engineers," the captain began her instructions by looking at the pair and directed her comments at them. "You should pay special attention to the lay of the land right around the ship where it is expected we will construct the building complex of our colony," Zawadi and Malcolm nodded in agreement. "You'll return to the ship for second mess."

Turning to the pair beside them, the captain continued, "After second mess, Gagandeep and Wan, the nutritionists, will go out and start collecting samples of the red groundcover. We'll need a preliminary analysis very soon to determine if the growth has any nutritional value, and just if and how it can be worked into our food supply. You will return to the ship for third mess." Gagandeep and Wan acknowledged the captain's orders.

John and Xia looked at each other and shifted nervously in their seats, knowing they were next. "John and Xia, the guardians, will go out after third mess and return at sunset," commanded the captain. "You have no specific duties that require you to be on the surface at this time, but you'll need to get used to it sooner or later."

"Now, Zawadi and Malcolm, if you'll follow the first officer, he'll take you to the disembarkation area, give you some equipment, and brief you on what to expect. Hoke, the flight engineer, is already out on the surface carrying out some routine inspections."

As the rest of the group broke up and returned to their quarters, Zawadi and Malcolm were led by the first officer through Level 2 to Level 3. From there, they went to an area not too far from the Landing Room. This area was filled with lockers, space suits, helmets, and all manner of other equipment. They were given a digital device that they both slipped on their wrists, which provided them with multiple readouts of local time, location, temperature, altitude, and humidity. It was also capable of detecting radiation and evaluation of atmospheric gasses and would sound an alarm if the environment began to become hazardous to human life. It also gave them access to Ana through a voice-activated communicator. If they wanted to talk directly with any of the others, Ana could also arrange for that.

The first officer gave them each a headpiece that had small nozzles hanging from it that fit into their nostrils. The tubes coming out of the nozzles were connected to a small cylinder, which was attached to a webbed belt around their waist. "This cylinder has an air mixture exactly like that of Earth. Kepler-438b's air mixture is slightly higher in oxygen level than that of Earth and of the air mixture you've been breathing on the ship. You'll get used to this, and, in fact, it should be a benefit to you doing physical labor of any kind. You should eventually enjoy more endurance than you have now," he explained. "But until you fully acclimate to the higher oxygen level, you might tend to become light-headed. If that happens, just insert the nozzles and turn this valve," he demonstrated on Zawadi's cylinder, "and stand quietly or sit down and breathe normally. Your head should clear in just a minute or two," he assured them. "Also, the surface is kind of soft and springy, like walking on cushions," he warned. "That too might take a little time to get used to, but at least there's one good thing about that..." he offered.

"What's that?" Malcolm opened his mouth and took the bait.

"It won't hurt much if you fall," laughed the first officer. "Remember, after you get situated out there, you should start doing some casual surveying of the site. We don't expect much from this morning's expedition, but you should at least start thinking about how you're going to survey and what equipment, including which robots, you'll initially require. The captain will want to start seeing your plans in a couple of days, so we can begin the offloading and disassembling of Ilithya-2 and move on to start the actual construction as soon as possible."

"Will do," responded Zawadi smartly as the first officer lead Malcolm and her to the pressure door on the side of the room. The flight engineer spun the wheel in the middle of the door to unseal and open it.

"We are just keeping this door closed as a precaution until we know more about the flora and fauna indigenous to our new home," he explained. "Nothing to be worried about. I'll make sure it's opened when it's time for you to return for second mess. If you need it opened before that, you can just ask Ana," he reminded them. "She can do that for you herself."

When the door was swung open, a draft of heavy, warm, humid air wafted over Zawadi and Malcolm. There was also an unfamiliar odor that was not altogether pleasant. "That smell is from the burned area made by our thrusters when we landed," offered the first officer. "Ana has confirmed that at this concentration, it is not at all toxic."

Zawadi and Malcolm stepped through the door onto the top of the landing ramp that led down to the surface. What lay before them was a gently rolling and seemingly unending expanse of low, red foliage extending from horizon to horizon. They slowly walked down the ramp and paused at the bottom.

"Ladies first," suggested Malcolm, bowing mockingly and gesturing for Zawadi to precede him. When she hesitated, he taunted, "Or would you like me to carry you over the threshold?"

Hearing that, Zawadi immediately stepped off the ramp and onto the planet's surface. She wobbled at first and grabbed back for Malcolm to keep her balance. "Wow!" she exclaimed. "This is like walking on an inflated mattress or a waterbed."

"A waterbed?" questioned Malcolm with obvious interest. "I'd like to hear more about your experiences on a waterbed sometime."

Zawadi ignored him. Slowly and very carefully, she began to move forward, away from the ramp. "Come on," she called, "it's not so bad once you get going."

Malcolm joined her, teetering a little at first, but soon they were walking side by side, circumnavigating Ilithya-2's landing site. The surface of the groundcover under the ship in the areas where the thrusters had been fired had been burned away during their landing. There was still groundcover there, no bare ground was visible, but the groundcover was blackened and was secreting some liquid that seemed to be the source of the unpleasant odor. They saw Hoke inspecting the base of a landing strut and waved. He acknowledged them by looking up but went right back to his work. When they reached the side of the landing site opposite the ramp and doorway, they stopped and began to survey the general area in more detail.

"There's no real advantage anywhere for the building sites that I can tell," offered Malcolm. "Every place looks pretty much the same, at least on the surface." Zawadi nodded, and Malcolm continued, "We'll need to find out how deep this groundcover is and what's underneath it: some probes, boring equipment, and even some ground-penetrating radar and sonar."

"Good idea," Zawadi agreed. "We should set up a grid around the ship, probably five-hundred meters square would be sufficient."

"Yes," said Malcolm as he squatted down and started digging into the groundcover with his hands. "It just looks like a tangled bunch of plants. Look here," he motioned to her, "the farther down you go, the lighter the red color gets, but," he grunted, "the tighter the bunching seems to be."

Zawadi examined the small hole he'd made and replied, "Well, we need to get down to bedrock for our foundations. Let's look around a little more and then return to the ship to start making a plan and a list of the equipment we'll need."

With that, they strolled the rest of the way around the ship, stopping just briefly at the strut Hoke had been inspecting. The strut itself had a large, wide, foot that was now embedded about one meter down into the groundcover. "It looks like this strut has struck bedrock," Zawadi remarked.

"Maybe, and maybe not," replied Malcolm. It might have just compressed the groundcover until it could support the weight of the ship. The footpad on the strut is fairly large. That could be it."

After they circled around to the ramp, they called Ana and requested she open the door. When they were inside, Ana closed and sealed it. After stowing their outside equipment, they headed back to their quarters to begin to draw up their plans for the very large task ahead of them.

At 12:00, they joined the others at second mess. Gagandeep and Wan were next to go outside and greeted them with a barrage of questions, all of which they deflected, suggesting they hold off on any detailed discussions until after Gagandeep and Wan, and later, John and Xia, had completed their initial visit to the surface. "That will be the time we should all sit down and compare notes," Zawadi suggested.

The first officer suddenly showed up, so Gagandeep and Wan ate quickly and were escorted by him to Level 3 and the disembarkation area. The first officer gave them the same tour he had given Zawadi and Malcolm, handed them their digital wrist communicators, and explained how to use the breathing-assist apparatus. He warned them about the surface texture and instructed them to use their time on the surface to start making plans to support their efforts as nutritionists of assuring the colony would have a constant, self-sustaining, and nutritional food supply. He reminded them they should try to incorporate as much native flora and fauna into food sources as possible. When their briefing was over, he sent them on their way down the landing ramp.

Although their initial challenges of walking on the groundcover were similar to the civil engineers, their focus, being nutritionists, was on locating native food sources. After scouting around the ship a bit, they both got down on their hands and knees to more closely examine this strange, but ubiquitous, groundcover.

"It all looks the same to me," offered Gagandeep. "Every area I've combed just seems to have the same type of plant. I haven't even seen any other organisms, like insects or worms."

"Me neither," agreed Wan. "And this red color, do you suppose that is something like a red chlorophyll?"

Gagandeep plucked a leaf-like terminus from the main body of the stem and pinched it hard between his thumb and the side of his index finger, rolling it so he could feel the texture. "It's very rubbery," he observed, "and look at the pinkish liquid secreting from where I tore it." He raised the pulp to his nose. "It has the same odor that greeted us when the door of the ship was opened, only not so pungent, not so unpleasant."

Wan plucked a leaf herself and did the same. "When we return tomorrow, we should gather up samples from various sites around the ship, and, of course, samples of anything else we find, and start breaking them down in the lab. We'll need samples of the leaves, stems, and roots if we can get down to them," said Wan.

"We can take some samples with us now," Gagandeep suggested.

"No, let's wait until tomorrow when we have a plan and bring the tools we'll need," Wan replied.

The two nutritionists moved back to the ramp, stopping only briefly to examine the burned areas. They agreed they'd need some samples from these damaged plants also. They stopped at the ramp and just stood together for a while before re-entering the ship, taking in the vista and enjoying the fresh air and Kepler-438's light filtering down through the clouds. It wasn't bright but certainly seemed adequate to promote plant growth and a refreshing change from the artificial light of the ship.

Third mess that evening was more lively. Zawadi and Malcolm seemed more willing to talk about their experience on the planet's surface, and Gagandeep and Wan were eager to join in. Only John and Xia had yet to be able to venture out of the ship, but that was about to change.

John and Xia were too excited to eat. The first officer did not make them wait long, however, and soon they had made the trek with him leading from the mess hall on Level 1 to the disembarkation area on Level 3. They listened attentively during the first officer's briefing and demonstrations. Their duties as guardians would be mainly performed in the nursery lab: bringing the zygotes out of cryo-suspension, monitoring them through their growth cycle, birthing, taking primary responsibility for, and directing the care of, the infants and toddlers, and nurturing them to adolescence. During their training on Earth, many of the other trainees in different disciplines teased them and had an alternate interpretation of their guardian "G" classification. They referred to them as "Glorified Nannies." "Glorified" or not, they felt they were the key to the success of these colonies whose sole mission was the proliferation of the human species throughout the universe.

When John and Xia stepped outside and made their way down the ramp, their perspective was much different than the other two pairs. They recognized the expanse of the soft, red surface as a great place for children to play. The lack of trees and streams was disappointing, but they shared their visions of structures that could provide shade and climbing challenges, of conduits with running water, and large, still, artificial ponds. Perhaps the nutritionists had brought some fish eggs or larva, although John remembered they said all they had were plant seeds. Maybe there was some native fauna living beneath the groundcover yet to be discovered. And birds! Yes, they both agreed the apparent absence of birds would be unfortunate, but they were sure they could make do somehow.

As they strolled around the ship, glad to be out in such an expanse of space and talking about what kind of facilities they'd eventually require to nurture the new crop of settlers from toddlers through young adulthood, they paused to talk with Hoke who was still probing the area around the sunken landing struts. The atmosphere of Kepler-438b was warm and humid. Hoke had unzipped his coveralls down to his waist, fully exposing his chest.

Xia's gaze lingered on Hoke's bronze and well-muscled physique, but something else caught John's attention. He maneuvered himself a little closer, stared intensely, and finally reached out and touched a pendant hanging from Hoke's neck.

"Hoke," he asked, "what's this pendant? It looks like the same image on the pendant Zawadi wears."

"Zawadi wears a pendant?" Hoke responded with guarded interest. "And you say the image looks like this one?"

"Well, yes," John hesitatingly replied, not wanting to

reveal too much about how he discovered that. "She told me it was an image of someone who helped liberate her people, or something like that."

"Did she give you a name?" Hoke continued with rising interest.

John hesitated, and then said, "Yes, but I forgot what it was. A short name, I think."

"Was it 'Atende?' " Hoke inquired timidly.

"Yes!" John immediately replied. "Yes, I think that was it. You should ask her, though, to be sure. Why would you both be wearing the same pendant?"

"Atende is an important person in my people's history also," Hoke offered. "And it does make sense that Zawadi would feel that way too."

"How is that possible?" countered Xia. "Zawadi's heritage is obviously African, whereas yours is, if I remember correctly, American Indian."

"Yes," acknowledged Hoke, "Shawnee to be specific, but there is a little-known historical connection between our two peoples."

"What could that be?" probed John.

"Well, that's a long story, and unimportant to our mission here. It's something we could discuss later after we've established a secure foothold. A story to be told around the campfire, you might say," Hoke replied half-jokingly. "But, I will ask Zawadi about her pendant. If what you say is true, it will mean a lot to both her and me. Thanks for the tip."

"Sure," John said, wondering what Zawadi would have to say about it all.

With that, John and Xia returned to the landing ramp, lingered there for a short time in the dimming light of the red dwarf star, Kepler-438, hidden by clouds and unseen as it slowly sunk below their new home's horizon. With the darkness came lights from the ship illuminating a circular area around it about two-hundred meters in diameter. By the time they walked up the well-lit landing ramp to the door, night had well and truly fallen on Kepler-438b.

Back inside, they found their comrades already firmly planted in the observation room impatiently taking turns describing their experiences outside, their discoveries, the obstacles they foresaw, the dreams they had, and most importantly, their plans on how best to make Kepler-438b their new home.

John and Xia eagerly joined them.

Chapter 7

Foothold

Over the next two days, the colonists spent most of their time preparing their reports to the captain with recommendations on how they wished to proceed in their areas. To do that, both the civil engineers and the nutritionists needed to spend the majority of their time on the planet's surface familiarizing themselves with Kepler-438b's terrain, conducting experiments, forming hypotheses, then testing and confirming these wherever possible. John and Xia, as guardians, had no less work to do in preparation for their report but did not have a need to venture out onto the planet's surface except for their own curiosity and pleasure.

Zawadi and Malcolm, the civil engineers, undoubtedly had the most work to do on the planet. They needed to analyze and discover the exact nature of the surface, specifically the depth of the groundcover, so they could hopefully find bedrock and move ahead with plans for erecting the foundations of the colony's structures. In doing so, they had a natural ally in Hoke who was concerned about the housing for the nuclear pile, the primary source of energy for the colony now, and for the foreseeable future.

The nuclear reactor itself, along with the sleeve of liquid hydrogen, should be protected within some kind of containment structure. Although the structure in which it was already housed was deemed adequate for interstellar flight, a planet's surface, where it would be vulnerable to all kinds of natural and man-made disasters including storms, floods, fires, earthquakes, sabotage, etc., deserved much more thought. The first choice would be to bury it deep in the ground, bedrock preferably, and seal it in. The electrical generators could also be buried under the surface just on top of the nuclear pile. The control areas could then be on or close to the surface, above the pile and the generators, and act as both a control and distribution point for the electrical energy to the various parts of the colony. Of course, research and experimentation would be done on alternate energy sources such as wind, solar, gravitation, and electrical fields, but the pile was expected to always be the "go-to" source.

Zawadi, Malcolm, and Hoke all three came to the mutual conclusion that the first order of business should be the excavation and construction of the containment area for the pile. The obvious place for this excavation was as directly under where the ship now stood as possible, so the pile, generators, and control facilities could then be lowered, re-configured, and sealed-in with the most efficiency and least chance of power disruption.

After sinking fifty probes to a depth of one hundred meters in a controlled grid pattern all around the area of the ship, they came to three conclusions:

1. Although the hardness, and therefore the integrity, of the groundcover increased with depth, no end to it was found.

2. At depths below twenty meters, the compacted groundcover afforded a hardness adequate to safely house the pile.
3. No place seemed to be any better suited than another.

Armed with that information, Hoke took the lead in preparing the report and recommendation for moving forward to relocate and secure the pile.

Zawadi and Malcolm had a slightly different set of challenges. They had a large greenhouse, domiciles, and a series of common areas also to build. They did not have the material to construct full foundations that extended twenty meters below the surface. They instead opted on a floating foundation that was designed to be used in sandy areas, such as desert, and could even be used on water. Their recommendations included modifying these prefabricated foundations slightly to adapt them to an anchoring system into Kepler-438b's persistent groundcover.

The three worked together to coordinate their reports, recommendations, and presentations in order to back each other up. When they presented them, the captain was impressed, and they were accepted by both the captain and first officer. An immediate go-ahead was given so that on the morning of the fourth day, they were to begin their first task: excavating a rectangular pit twenty meters on each side and forty meters deep beneath the center of the ship directly under the current housing for the pile.

Early on the first day of their research, and at the first opportunity he had to be alone with Zawadi, Hoke recounted his previous chance discussion with John and showed her his pendant. Upon seeing the pendant, Zawadi immediately threw her arms around Hoke and broke down in tears of joy. They sat holding hands for a long while, each knowing that this was the start of a very special relationship.

Wan and Gagandeep's, the nutritionists, research was of an entirely different nature. It first consisted of scouring the planet's surface around Ilithya-2 with the intention of collecting samples of all the flora and fauna they encountered. They ventured out as far as five kilometers in three directions from the ship. They did so all on foot. They found if they skipped along the surface of the groundcover, it was springy enough to help propel them on their way. When they demonstrated this gait to the other colonists and crew members, they all had a good laugh, but all immediately adopted the technique. They would take samples from the surface to one meter deep. During these initial days of research, they collected over five-hundred samples, all sealed, tagged, and documented, but found not one trace of any other living organism besides the groundcover, or even of any other inorganic material, for that matter.

Although this lack of diversity was troubling, it at least gave them the opportunity to focus all their efforts on the groundcover itself. The plant, or whatever it was, upon close inspection, was fairly unremarkable. It was very durable and did exhibit some variation in size and even color of the termini, but generally, all the samples seemed pretty much the same.

Kepler-438b Groundcover Termini
Actual Size x 10

Every afternoon after a half-day of collecting, they would return to the ship, and with the doctor and Ana's help, would start examining the samples. They had a structured and rigorous routine. First, they would examine them for contaminants. They never found any. Nothing was ever discovered other than the groundcover itself. Then they would separate the samples into three specimens: one to test for toxicity to humans, one to determine the nutritional value, and one for DNA analysis. The results of these tests were both astounding and puzzling.

The groundcover showed no signs of toxicity. Even when crushed, the pinkish, liquid discharge seemed to have no real characteristic differences from the rest of the plant itself. The red coloring did come from a biomolecule very similar to Earth's green chlorophyll and did have the same function, the enabling of photosynthesis. Green chlorophyll absorbs light most strongly in the blue portion of the electromagnetic spectrum but is a poor absorber in the green and near-green portions of the spectrum. This is why most chlorophyll-containing tissues on Earth are green. There are some instances of red chlorophyll, but they are mainly found in marine plants at great depths where the light spectrum has been severely weakened and distorted. The star Kepler-438, in spite of its reddish glow, emits light primarily in the green and near-green portions of the electromagnetic spectrum, making a red biomolecule much more efficient at absorbing its light energy and promoting photosynthesis.

The plant had amazing nutritional attributes. These were most present in the termini: the topmost, reddish, leaf-like structures; and less so in the paler, stem-like structures which came from below the surface. In fact, at a depth of about one meter, the groundcover ceased having any detectable nutritional value at all. This discovery was not only essential in establishing the groundcover as a food source but also indicated its harvesting would be relatively easy since the best food value was from the portions near the surface.

The DNA analysis was puzzling, however. Ana had already confirmed that the groundcover could not be neatly placed in either the normal Earth animal or plant categories. Although it had fairly classic DNA, the double-helix structure and the four nucleotides: adenine, thymine, guanine, and cytosine, it had a fifth, heretofore undiscovered, nucleotide. In Earth DNA, each of the nucleotide pairs only with one other: adenine pairs with thymine while guanine pairs with cytosine. In the groundcover's DNA, the fifth nucleotide, which was promptly christened "keplerine," seemed to be like a wild card. It could and would pair with any of the other four nucleotides. Its purpose and the ramifications of such pairings were, at this point, unknown. Keplerine was, under laboratory conditions anyway, found to be as easily digestible as the other nucleotides, and like them, could be efficiently assimilated by the human body as a food source.

The other odd discovery was the DNA analysis from all samples produced exactly the same results. All samples, no matter what location or how deep they were extracted, were exactly the same. On Earth, not only every species has their own DNA pattern, but every individual within that species has a unique DNA pattern. In fact, even within an individual, it is possible to have slight DNA variations within different systems and organs. The fact that all the DNA was exactly the same could lead to a conclusion that not only was all of Kepler-438b's groundcover the same species of organism, it might just all be the same organism: one single organism covering the entire planet! This hypothesis was certainly "food for thought," as the ever-punning doctor put it.

When presenting their very promising findings to the captain and the first officer, Wan and Gagandeep included in their recommendations that several drones be fitted to travel to more distant areas of the planet to obtain samples for further study. The captain was, of course, delighted with their finding that the plentiful groundcover could be a ready source of food. She also consented to their request for further research involving drones but gave this task a low priority.

Their main takeaway from the meeting with the captain and the first officer was that their first priority now, and the next challenge was to conduct actual human nutritional testing. At least one of them was going to have to volunteer to go on a strict diet of groundcover. Who that would be was left up to them to decide.

As guardians, John and Xia's exploration, preparation, and recommendations were almost exclusively academic. They spent almost every hour of every day with Lyuba, the cyberneticist, probing Ana for details of human fetal development, especially under abnormal circumstances and in artificial wombs. There was a lot of literature in this field, and it had to be sorted through to determine what might be useful and what not. Also, Lyuba was scheduled to help them set up the computer-assisted schooling for the young colonists beginning at the age of three through their sixteenth birthday. The core curriculum had already been set, but references to the historical events that had occurred since then would have to be added. Also, there would be a need for new syllabi for practical skills needed on Kepler-438b, such as maintaining the equipment and husbandry of the food sources. These would have to be developed. Some of these would have to wait years until the nutritionists were much farther along in their mission, and the colony was more settled, but preparing the templates could begin now.

John especially enjoyed working with Lyuba because he knew she held the keys to Ana's deepest secrets. He was thinking too much like a human when he hoped Ana would associate him more closely with Lyuba and be a little freer in granting him access to some of the information he had been seeking. Ana might utilize analog processing in the foreground, but her fundamental processes were still rooted firmly in the digital world. That meant rules were rules with no exceptions for fuzzy logic and ambiguous concepts like "friend." For the most part,

John and Xia's actual work was pretty much on hold until Zawadi and Malcolm completed the construction of their laboratory and nursery, and all the zygotes and other equipment could be relocated there.

On the morning of the fourth day since landing, Hoke, Zawadi, and Malcolm were up and out early, unloading two, large, excavation robots. These robots were mobile, and each had a laser-cutting system to break up the area to be excavated into small, more easily handled pieces, and a shoveling tool to gather the pieces and place them in a transport vehicle or waste site. In this case, the waste vehicles were four large, truck-like robots capable of transporting large containers. All the robots and vehicles had been fitted with tracks instead of wheels, although most of the larger robots already had tracks as standard gear.

It took about an hour to get everything set up. The surveying had already been done as had a site been chosen to dump the contents of the excavation. That site was about five kilometers from the excavation site. This was a long way, but this site would be needed for other waste in the future. It was thought that would be far enough from the colony so there would be no interference with any other activities and could serve as their permanent waste site.

When the excavation finally got underway, several large robots began lasering around the edges of the containment pit and slicing the surface into one-meter cubes. The cubes were then scooped up several at a time by the shoveling tool and deposited in the first of the waiting transport robots. When all the cubes in this first layer had been removed, the transport robot began its five-kilometer journey to the waste disposal site, and another transport robot took its place at the side of the excavation. The excavation robots repeated the lasering and removal process, loading up the second transport robot. Each cycle took about forty-five minutes, planet-time, so the four transport robots were easily able to drive the five kilometers to the waste site, dump their load, and return in time to take their place in line for another load.

Since the depth of the containment pit for the nuclear pile was to be forty meters, the entire excavation would take at least twenty hours. The doctor, Zawadi, and Malcolm had set up five-hour shifts to oversee the operation. This would allow them to work for five hours and have ten hours off. They were always all on-call, of course, should a problem arise. None did, but the cutting process did take appreciably longer the deeper they went. Instead of taking forty-five minutes for each layer, the last ten layers took almost double that time.

At dawn on the fifth day, however, the excavation had been completed. A few odds and ends needed cleaning up, but after second mess, the pit was ready to fit with the forms which would be filled with a recently developed non-organic, polymer that is a completely synthetic hybrid clone of the semi-organic polyetheretherketone and polyetherimide polymers. This new polymer combined the human biocompatibility of the former with the formidable tensile strength of the latter to form the virtually impervious fifty-centimeter-thick walls of the subterranean containment area. All this was accomplished using the robots well before third mess, and the polymer was injected just as Kepler-438's light was waning. All would be ready the next morning for the clearing of the forms and the physical relocation of the nuclear pile, the generators, and the control area into their respective levels of the containment pit.

Third mess that evening presented what was going to prove to be a continuing pattern. Zawadi and Hoke sat together. Their dining consisted of mostly idle talk but was punctuated with sporadic bursts of laughter. Malcolm, sensing the growing intimate bond between the two, moved tables to sit with Wan and Gagandeep. The interaction there was mainly between Malcolm and Gagandeep, Wan, voluntarily or involuntarily, assuming the role of an observer. John and Xia still dined together but would often include Lyuba at their table. Their interactions were pleasant but mainly mission-oriented. The captain and the first officer were seldom present at mess, but when they were, they always sat together, ate quickly in silence, and left as soon as they were done. The doctor always dined alone.

While Zawadi, Malcolm, and Hoke were excavating the site for the containment area, Wan, Gagandeep, and the doctor were wrestling with their last orders from the captain. She demanded a human trial to prove the viability of introducing the groundcover as a staple in the colonists' diet. Who would it be?

None of the three immediately volunteered. The doctor, half-seriously and half-jokingly, suggested Malcolm, with or without his knowledge, but Gagandeep immediately vetoed that, and Wan backed him. They needed to conduct this test out in the open for many reasons, not just ethical ones. They needed the test to be very public and transparent to engender the confidence of their fellow colonists. In fact, their goal was not just to convince the colony that the groundcover was a viable food source, but actually present it in such a way that it was seen as a very desirable choice.

Finally, Gagandeep volunteered to be the human guinea pig. They quickly drew up some plans and a sequence of tests. The initial steps would be separated by a period of four hours or more to allow for any adverse reactions.

The first test would be smearing the juice from the raw, crushed plant on his skin. After four hours with no reaction, they moved on to the second test, which was touching the pulp to his lips. After success there, they then placed the pulp in his mouth for a few seconds. The final two steps in this phase were chewing and then swallowing. These last steps were done in the evening, so any effects would have a full eight hours overnight to show themselves. Gagandeep did not sleep well that night, but he did survive with no incident.

These tests were repeated with different parts of the groundcover: the termini (leaves), tendrils, stalks both shallow and deep, but other than the termini, all were either too tasteless or too tough to be considered as an everyday food source.

After these tests, the group moved on to cooking the groundcover termini. It was boiled, steamed, poached, baked, braised, roasted, grilled, seared, pan-fried, deep-fried, etc....; there seemed no end to the techniques that Ana would find and present to them. Gagandeep tried them all, and all proved to be not only palatable, but some, actually delicious.

The other colonists were continually briefed on what was taking place. Gagandeep quickly became the center of everyone's attention during their meals and evenings. They all had but one question for him, "What did it taste like?"

The doctor had anticipated this and tried to convince Gagandeep to answer, "chicken," but Gagandeep either was not familiar with the joke or wanted to give this very important experiment the respect he felt it deserved. After several days of eating both raw and cooked groundcover, however, he did have an answer which he revealed in the observation room where they all still met after third mess to discuss their day's work.

"It tastes like fish," he unexpectedly blurted out. "It tastes like a mild, ocean fish. The fish I have eaten that comes the closest to it would be cod, or maybe halibut." They all rushed to crowd around him. "But it has more of the consistency of squid," he continued pleased with all the attention. "Not so rubbery as squid, but more substantial than raw fish." This revelation set off a cacophony of raucous shouts and laughter.

"So," interjected Malcolm when the laughter had died down somewhat, "when are we all going to get a chance to try this delicacy?"

"Soon," replied Gagandeep, "very soon. In fact, Wan has an announcement about that very thing."

All eyes shifted to Wan. "Yes," Wan shyly responded, "Actually, we need your help. We'd like each of you to recommend a recipe that would feature the groundcover. It can be used as a vegetable, a meat, or a fish. It seems to be very versatile," she continued gathering confidence as she went. "You might all consider a recipe that reflects your ethnic background. We thought that would be fun." Everyone cooed and nodded in agreement. "Lyuba has assured us that Ana can create simulations of whatever spices or sauces you would require. What we've decided we'll do is stage a contest." This brought even more ooh's and ah's from the group. "We'll pick a night and have all the dishes prepared for third mess. Everyone can sample every dish, and the dish with the most votes will win!" Wan ended her soliloquy on a high note.

"What will we win?" Malcolm teased, "A lifetime's supply of groundcover?" Everyone burst out laughing at this one, and the jubilant atmosphere continued throughout the rest of the evening. It was a much-needed respite from the constant pressure being applied by the captain.

As John and Xia left the room, Xia whispered in his ear, "If it tastes anything like fish, I know the perfect Chinese dish to enter in the contest." John seemed uninterested, but Xia pressed on about it, "I'll start researching it with Ana immediately." John smiled but said nothing in return.

Xia, John, and Lyuba had been working literally day and night making sure all the i's were dotted and the t's were crossed on their report and recommendations to the captain. Participating in all the discussions in the observation room after their work made them anticipate finding some unusual and important alterations they'd have to make to their plans as guardians, but so far, the only real difference was the quantity of zygotes they'd have to nurture through adolescence. The best they could come up with were some schedules that extended the entire process out over thirty-two years, Earth-years. They were still not used to thinking in the Kepler-438b time frame.

After the initial four zygotes, the plan would allow for sixteen new colonists to begin their life every year. That certainly sounded like a handful, and they added provisions for support from Lyuba, the doctor, and even the captain and first officer. They slotted in some ad-hoc, volunteer duties for any other colonists who could lend a hand from time to time. The plan was constructed to provide new generations of colonists that would cover all the skillsets now known to be critical for maintenance of the colony, and placeholders for skillsets yet to be identified. In the end, all three were satisfied with the report and looked forward to their upcoming audience with the captain.

The captain, however, seemed to become very busy and kept putting off their presentation. The work of the civil engineers and the nutritionists was more pressing, they knew, but these delays were somewhat dispiriting. Right after one of the delays, Hoke came to see them and asked if one of them could assist his group by accompanying a pair of robots out to the waste site and oversee its incineration. The pile of waste now accumulated from the twenty- by twenty- by forty-meter containment pit was at least sixteen thousand cubic meters, and also, there were other waste items that had been deposited there by the other colonists and crew. John immediately agreed to help and asked both Xia and Lyuba to accompany him. Lyuba declined, saying she had some finishing touches to put on her part of the presentation, but Xia eagerly volunteered to go with him.

"Sure, I could use the exercise and fresh air," she asserted. "I'd like to get out in the sunlight too, even if it is always cloudy. If I'm going to live here the rest of my life, I might as well learn to enjoy it."

"Sounds good to me," replied John. "Let's go."

They went with Hoke to the disembarkation room and put on their equipment while he briefed them on their assignment. They were to accompany two robots who would have an array of lasers that would organize and incinerate the waste. The robots would first comb through the waste slicing up any large chunks into smaller pieces, then shoving the waste into a compact pile, and finally incinerate the waste with a series of overlapping laser sweeps. John and Xia were to travel in two separate, small transport bots and position themselves at a safe distance from the waste. They would observe and assist if necessary but were instructed to call Hoke if there was even a hint of irregularities.

"What about the groundcover?" John asked. "Is it at all flammable?"

"No, we tested that thoroughly," assured Hoke. "When parts of the groundcover are separated from the bunch, they start to deteriorate pretty rapidly. They stiffen, become black, and eventually do become flammable, but are not very volatile. That should be of no concern today."

"Okay," added Xia, "we'll call you when we get there, and before we allow the robots to begin the laser sweeps."

"Great," acknowledged Hoke.

John and Xia found their two individual transport bots waiting for them at the bottom of the ramp. The other two robots were just ahead of them and had already started their slow drive to the waste site. There was a path already worn in the groundcover that showed them the way. The groundcover on the path was turning a dirty, reddish-black from being crushed by the many trips made to transport the waste from the containment pit. The pace was slow in the tracked vehicles, but they arrived at the waste site in less than twenty minutes. On the way, John and Xia had their transport bots moving next to each other so they could talk. It was small talk, mainly about their mission and the specific roles they would be expected to play. The terrain, although exotic and beautiful at first, quickly became monotonous and unappealing. They saw the mounds at the waste site rising up above the general terrain from more than a kilometer away. By the time they'd arrived, the two lead robots were already at work attempting to break up and corral the waste into a more manageable, single pile. That took less than fifteen minutes. During that time, John and Wan repositioned their transport bots to a safe distance, and on top of the highest point they could find, which was about twenty meters from the waste pile and out of the line-of-sight for the laser arrays.

When the robots had finished their preparation of the waste pile, John called Hoke, "We're ready to go here. I'm going to give the command to the robots to position themselves away from the pile and light it up," he reported.

"Okay," replied Hoke, "and just be sure you keep your distance, but there shouldn't be any problems. In fact, the small amounts of waste we've tried to incinerate before were hard to completely disintegrate. You might have to watch for that," he warned.

"We will," promised John. "We'll call you before we start heading back."

With that, John gave the robots the command to finish their preparation, retreat to a safe distance of ten meters, and charge their lasers. When that was done, he ordered the laser arrays to begin firing.

The incineration started slowly. The already blackened groundcover began to shrivel and smoke. As the laser sweeps spread across the pile, a shimmering, translucent, gray sheen started rising from the smoking heap. As the sheen became darker and much thicker, John called Hoke again to check-in.

"Hey! There are a lot of emissions, or smoke, or something here. Is that normal?" he asked.

"Yes," assured Hoke, "yes, it is. And stay away from it.

It's very acrid and smells horrible," he added. "I hope Wan and Gagandeep have better luck cooking the groundcover than we did incinerating it. If it tastes like this smoke smells, I'd rather starve," he quipped.

John decided they should move their transport bots back a little just to be sure. He said as much to Xia and moved his back about ten more meters. When Zia attempted to coax her transport bot into a tight U-turn, one of the tracks dug in and became entangled in the groundcover. The bot became stuck. Just then, the breeze must have shifted because they were suddenly engulfed by the shimmering, thick, acrid vapor from the smoldering heap.

The last thing John saw clearly was Xia furiously trying to free her transport bot. The sheen hit him like a wall, a wall of acid. He'd never been maced before, but he thought this is what that must feel like. His skin, eyes, and nose all felt like they were on fire. His eyes were watering so badly he couldn't see two feet in front of him. He immediately grabbed at his headpiece and fumbled around until he found the air nozzles. He inserted them into his nostrils and opened the valve of the canister attached to his waist while he leaped out of his bot and headed straight for Xia. She was only ten meters away, but he could barely make her out in the shimmering vapor. In spite of the fresh air assist, his lungs were burning. He could feel himself losing consciousness. He kept calling out to Xia but got no answer. Finally, he stumbled and fell. The last thing he remembered was tapping the digital communicator on his wrist and croaking, "Hoke! Hoke!" Then everything went black.

Hoke didn't hear John's actual calls for help. They were relayed to him by Ana. She contacted him with an alarm, advised him of the emergency, and played back John's last transmission. Hoke's first instinct was to take off running to the waste site. He knew he could run that distance, five kilometers, faster than a transport bot, so without further considerations, he immediately set off. As he ran, he instructed Ana to sound the general alarm, call Zawadi and Malcolm for help, and bring them completely up to date. He also instructed Ana to contact the captain, the doctor, and everyone available to prepare to receive injured personnel. He advised Ana he would report in as soon as he knew more.

Hoke found running on Kepler-438b very easy. The groundcover gave way a little under his strides but rebounded to help spring him forward. The high percentage of oxygen also helped him with his stamina. He easily covered the five kilometers in just over ten minutes.

When Hoke arrived at the waste site, he saw both John and Xia lying next to one of the transport bots. Xia seemed to have fallen out of her bot, and John appeared to be reaching out for her. Both were unconscious but alive. Other than that, there was no clue as to what had happened. The incinerator bots had finished their job and were standing motionless waiting for their next command. John's transport bot was off to the side a bit, but all appeared to be in working order. The only thing of note which was discovered later was that one of the tracks on Xia's bot had been locked up in the groundcover. There was, of course, the nasty stench of burning groundcover, but that had been expected. Hoke had no idea what had happened.

He contacted the doctor and relayed as much situational detail as he could. He carefully loaded both John and Xia aboard the one working transport bot and started back towards the ship. He soon met Zawadi and Malcolm, and they helped him return the unconscious colonists to the ship. Once there, they were rushed into the medical facilities where the doctor was waiting. He had prepared for the worst.

Chapter 8

Settling In

John became slowly aware that he was lying on his back, staring up at the jungle canopy. Dark shadows enveloped everything. He tried to sit up but found he couldn't move. He could hear the murmuring of the stream in the distance, and now and then the call of a bird or the scuff of something unseen moving through the underbrush. Twice he thought he "saw" lights in the distance, but felt them more than saw them. He seemed to go in and out of his dream-like consciousness, like a heavy log bobbing up and down in the water. Suddenly, a sharp pain shot up his arm, and his head starting buzzing like it had been asleep...

"I think he's waking up," said the doctor. He stood back and declared proudly, "That shot of adrenalin must have done the trick."

Lyuba leaned forward, putting her face directly above John's and called softly, "John, John. Can you hear me? It's Lyuba."

John struggled to extricate himself from his dream. He was half-in and half-out. "Xia," was all he could manage to say.

"John!" called Lyuba a little more forcefully. "Wake

up! Come back to us! Tell me you see me."

John reluctantly opened his eyes but immediately closed them in reaction to the bright lights. "Xia?" was all he could manage.

"Lyuba!" Lyuba corrected. "I'm Lyuba. Xia's in the next room. She's okay. She wants to see you. We've all been waiting for you to wake up."

John opened his eyes again, this time in a tight squint. "Xia?" he repeated. He turned his head to the side a little and made a fist with his right hand. It felt good to be able to move again. He turned his head again and saw Lyuba and the doctor. "Hi," he said softly. "Yes, I'm here now. I'm back."

Lyuba threw herself on him and gave him a big hug. "I knew it! I knew it!" she kept repeating. "I knew he'd be okay."

"Well, you just might have to thank me a little for that," reminded the doctor.

"Yes! Yes!" exclaimed Lyuba and hugged him also. "Ana!" she happily commanded, "Tell the others! Tell them John has regained consciousness."

The doctor moved past Lyuba to examine John. He checked his eyes for pupil response and took his pulse and blood pressure. Taking into consideration the shot of adrenalin, everything seemed okay, certainly within normal limits. "How do you feel?" he asked him.

"Groggy," said John. "Very groggy, but jittery. Like I've slept for a month and just drank a pot of coffee."

"Well," said the doctor with a laugh, "you almost have slept for a month. You've been in a coma for ten days now. The last couple of days, you've shown signs of waking up, so this morning I decided to help you along with a wee shot of adrenalin. It seems to have worked," he chuckled. "That's the pot of coffee you feel."

"Whoa!" moaned John. "Ten days? What about Xia? How's Xia?" he asked worriedly.

"Xia's fine," said the doctor in a more sober tone. "She's right next door and resting comfortably."

"Is she conscious?" queried John.

"Yes. In fact, she regained consciousness three days ago, well before you," reported the doctor.

"Can I see her?" John implored.

"No, not right now. I want to run some more tests on you first," cautioned the doctor. "I want to make sure you don't have any residual effects that might endanger her. Maybe tonight, if all goes well," he added. "Can you sit up for me?"

John gingerly sat up and looked around. The doctor started thumping on his chest and back, asking him to take deep breaths.

"How's that?" the doctor asked. "Do you think you can breathe, okay?"

"Yes," replied John. "The last thing I remember though, was breathing in that awful vapor from the groundcover."

"Yes, we know," affirmed the doctor. "We pieced together your and Xia's last minutes from what was found at the site and some logs Ana extracted from both your communicators and the robots. We've also since tested the lasering of the groundcover and were able to reproduce that acrid, translucent vapor you inhaled." The doctor moved on, taking John's temperature while pushing and probing other areas. "Nasty stuff, that," the doctor added ominously.

John had blood drawn several times. He was allowed to get up and walk around his room with help from Lyuba and underwent a variety of tests throughout the day. When it was time for second mess, he was given a glass of the doctor's infamous nutritional liquid. "Not again," was John's reaction. The doctor took that as a good sign.

Just before third mess, John's room filled up with some cheerful visitors. Led by Zawadi, all the colonists were there, hugging John and shaking his hand, welcoming him back. Only the captain and first officer were missing, but they had earlier sent their regards via a hologram.

John accepted all the attention for about ten minutes and then asked, "How about Xia? When can I see her?"

The room fell silent, and the doctor stepped forward. "We can all go see Xia right now," he replied. "Let's go," he said as he motioned to everyone to clear the room. As they were filing out, the doctor added, "but first, Zawadi has something to tell you." John looked at Zawadi. There was both joy and sadness in her eyes.

"Zawadi," he pleaded, "what's wrong?"

"I'm so glad to see you back and well," began Zawadi. "Xia regained consciousness a couple days ago, and we were all very happy, of course, but that happiness couldn't be complete until you returned also."

"And?" John prompted.

"And...," Zawadi continued haltingly, "...and Xia will be so happy to see you too."

"And?" John demanded now getting annoyed with this cat-and-mouse game.

Zawadi took a deep breath, "Xia's not fully recovered," she said cautiously.

"How so?" questioned John.

"Xia..., Xia can't speak, or at least won't speak."

"What? Xia won't speak?" John asked incredulously.

"...or can't," Zawadi continued, "The doctor's not sure which. Anyway, she doesn't speak."

John just sat on the side of his bed, staring at the wall.

"She seems to understand everything," Zawadi quickly added with a more optimistic tone, "She's a little confused sometimes, and, of course, very quiet, but mostly she just doesn't talk."

John stared at the wall a little longer, then cleared his throat and slid off the bed onto the floor. "Well then, let's go see her."

Zawadi held John's arm as he shuffled out of his room, across the hall, and into Xia's. Her room was full of the colonists, and they all cheered when he entered.

"See! Here he is! We told you he'd be okay," said Malcolm.

Xia was sitting up in her bed and straining to catch a glimpse of John through the assembled group. When she did, her face lit up, and she broke out into a very big smile. She stretched out her arms to John, and when they first embraced, she started sobbing uncontrollably. The doctor quickly moved in to separate them, but Xia held on to John as if her life depended on it.

"It's okay," John kept repeating, "It's okay now, Xia. I'm here. I'm here now, and I'll never leave you again."

"Let's give these two some privacy," suggested Zawadi. With that, the group, one by one, went over to John and Xia, smiled and touched them, then left.

The doctor was the last one out the door, but before he left, he promised, "I'll be right outside if you need me." With that, he closed the door, and they were alone.

John and Xia just sat on the bed, looking at each other. Xia's eyes still radiated that warmth that had first attracted John to her. They both smiled. "Xia," John finally ventured a question, "how are you? How have you been?" Xia smiled and nodded her head up and down slightly as if to signal things were okay. "They say you won't talk. Why is that?" John pressed on.

Xia's smile dimmed a little, and she looked away, up towards the corner of the room. When she looked back, her smile returned, and she took John's hand and pressed it against her cheek. She gazed intently into his eyes.

"No problem," John finally said, "We were always able to communicate without a lot of words anyway."

Xia lay back on her bed, still holding John's hand close to her face. Her eyes fluttered a bit, closed, and she quickly fell asleep.

John sat with her there for a long while. When he was sure she was fully asleep, he carefully pulled back his hand and stood by the bed. He slowly moved out of the room, into the corridor, and went to look for the doctor. He was in the room right next door and looked up in surprise when John entered.

"What's happened to her?" John asked.

"Nothing critical," the doctor assured him. "I think all this might be temporary. She has improved somewhat in just the few days since she's come around. Her balance has returned, and she seems more alert every day."

"Her balance? What do you mean 'her balance has returned?' "

"When she first came to, she couldn't even sit up without assistance, much less walk. Now, just in two days, she can sit up, get out of bed, and walk around her room — with some assistance of course," he added.

"How about her speech?" John pressed on, "Why can't she talk?"

"I haven't been able to find any physical reason for her lack of speech. I don't know so much if she can't talk as she won't talk. Maybe she forgot how or temporarily lost the ability, or maybe she just doesn't want to."

"Why is she so much more affected than me?"

"Again, I don't really know," the doctor admitted, "I'm running all the tests Ana, and I can come up with to find out just what happened to her. Comparing them to test results from you might now help me discover differences, anomalies. As to the 'why,' I can only assume it's either just a difference in the way your bodies reacted to the vapors or, more likely, because you did use your breathing assist tubes. When Hoke found you, he did say you were wearing yours, and it had been turned on."

John tried to remember but could not. "The last thing I remember was arriving at the waste site. Everything was fine then," he said, "and then there was the horrible smell."

"Yes, that's normal. Some more of your memory may return in time – or may not," the doctor advised. "In any event, you're here now, and from all I've seen and the tests I've run so far, you seem generally fine."

"I feel completely exhausted," John confided.

"Yes, I imagine so. Why don't we return to your room so you can rest? That would be best, in fact, you can consider that 'doctor's orders!' " he exclaimed, emphasizing the last phrase to try to lighten the mood.

John returned to his room and fell into a dreamless sleep as soon as his head hit the pillow. It must have been a very deep sleep, too, because when he awoke, he was in a different, larger room. Xia lay asleep in a bed next to his. Lyuba was sitting on a bench near the door, pecking away at her e-tablet.

"Hi," John said weakly.

"Hi," Lyuba acknowledged while putting down her e-tablet and moving over to his bedside. She put her hand on his forehead as if she were testing for a fever. "How are you feeling?"

"Okay, I guess," replied John. "I was going to say, 'I've had worse,' but I'm not sure if I ever did have anything worse than this happen," he added, with a hint of a smile.

Lyuba smiled back.

John rolled onto his side, facing Xia, and asked quietly, "Why is Xia here?"

Lyuba explained, "After you'd left her room last night, she awoke and became very agitated to discover you had gone. She thrashed about on her bed and kept trying to get up. The doctor finally ordered the two of you to be relocated into this room. She quieted down as soon as she saw you. It looks like you're going to be stuck with her."

"Good," declared John. "That's the way I want it too. We've come this far together, and we should be together now, and stay together into whatever the future holds for us."

Lyuba nodded her agreement, but the corners of her mouth revealed a hint of disappointment.

* * * *

Over the next week, John and Xia convalesced in their room. With each day, John grew stronger, but Xia's overall condition did not improve as rapidly. She could function reasonably well, and even care for herself, but still seemed to be confused a lot and, of course, would not speak. Psychologically, she continued to be very dependent upon John, a situation that John not only accepted but seemed to embrace.

The rest of the colonists were moving right along with their tasks but always found time in the mornings and evenings to pay John and Xia a visit. On one of those visits, Zawadi and Malcolm gave a detailed report of their handiwork aided by an image of the almost-completed compound.

"Ana, display the image of the compound," commanded Zawadi. A crisp hologram was projected in the middle of the room between John and Xia's beds. "Here it is," Zawadi proudly announced, "courtesy of the big guy, Hoke, and one of his surveillance drones."

Image of Compound

Zawadi moved through the hologram and sat down on John's bed. Malcolm followed and stood by Xia's. "As you know, all the structures were taken almost as-is from Ilithya-2. She was designed not only to bring us here safely but to also be the source of all the mostly prefabricated structures for our new home. The long, glass area here at the front is the greenhouse. Wan and Gagandeep are already hard at work planting seedlings to supplement our diet. One can't live on groundcover alone, you know," she added with a wink.

"The sets of buildings sprouting out at right angles on either side of the main corridor just behind the greenhouse are workrooms and storage areas. Our robots and other tools are all stored there. The tower just above them contains our water extractor, and the water is stored in the tanks to the far right. This all seems to be working well." She paused for questions. None coming, she continued. "The main housing units are on the ground floor of the big dome. That's where you and Xia will be living as soon as you can convince the doctor to let you out of here."

John looked at Xia and smiled, "I hope that will be very soon," he replied. "We ask him about that every day.

"The pair of structures jutting out at right angles from the middle of the dome, just here," Zawadi pointed, "contain the labs to the left and the hospital on the right. All your zygotes are here," she continued as she pointed to the topmost set of structures, "and the hospital is here," she said, gesturing at the bottom set. "In fact, we are all right here, right now," Zawadi declared as she pointed to the last structure on the bottom set.

John and Xia both scooted closer to the hologram to get a better view of their location. "What else is in the dome?" John queried.

"The dome is the main structure," Malcolm explained. "Beneath it and three levels down is the containment area for the pile, the nuclear reactor. The electrical generators and the control areas are on top of that in sub-level two and sub-level one. Also, with our living units on ground-level one, are the community areas, food preparation, and even the old mess hall!" Malcolm added with a wink. Both John and Xia seemed pleased with that.

"The second level of the dome contains the domiciles and offices for the crew: the captain, first officer, doctor, and Hoke," Zawadi stated with a sly smile.

"And above that, in the third, top level, is the domicile for the minister and his wife," added Malcolm.

"Who?" John demanded, while getting out of his bed,

"Who? What minister?"

Zawadi cast a disapproving glare at Malcolm and replied, "The minister for the One World Government. The minister MM-2, and his wife MF-2. That's one mystery that was solved while you two were on vacation."

"They were the two humans in cryo?" John asked incredulously. "Ministers stowed away on our ship?"

"Yes," Zawadi confirmed. "The doctor revived them as soon as we had their quarters completed. That was less than a week ago."

"They've been up there ever since," Malcolm added, "I've only seen them once when the doctor brought them to third mess to introduce them, and then they didn't say anything, just smiled and waved," Malcolm said disgustedly, "like typical politicians."

"What is their function here?" asked John.

"Who knows?" replied Malcolm, "Who even knows what their function was on Earth?" he added sarcastically. "If it was to govern and take care of us all, they certainly didn't do a very good job of that, now did they?"

An awkward silence conveyed agreement.

"The doctor says they'll become more active and involved with the colony once they recuperate from their cryo. We can all sympathize with that," reminded Zawadi. "Anyway, they are said to be coming to third mess tomorrow night when Wan and Gagandeep are having their 'Groundcover Recipe Challenge' as a kind of celebration marking our official moves into our permanent domiciles in the dome. We've already checked with the doctor, and he's said you two can come. That's the news we've all been waiting for!" Zawadi cheerfully announced.

"Great!" responded John, "Don't you think that's good news?" he asked, turning to Xia. She smiled broadly and nodded her head in agreement.

As soon as Zawadi and Malcolm left, John moved over to Xia and asked, "So what are you going to fix for the recipe challenge?" Xia looked surprised and just shook her head no. "What do you mean, 'no?' " John countered, "I remember when the contest was first announced, you were all excited about some Chinese recipe. Ana," John pressed on, "do you recall Xia's research on a recipe for this challenge?"

"Of course," Ana replied.

"Please project the results," John requested.

Xia's Recipe

Steamed Fish with Sweet and Sour Sauce
Ingredients:
— Two small sea bream or other white fish meat
— 1 tbsp wine
— 1 tsp salt
— 1 tsp ginger juice
— 1 small green pepper, seeded and diced
— 2 red peppers, cut into small pieces
— 4 slices of ginger
— 1 tbsp sliced cucumber pickle
— 2 tbsp oil
— 2 tbsp vinegar
— 2 tbsp sugar
— 1 tbsp soy sauce
— 2 tbsp sesame oil
— 2 tsp cornstarch
— 1 cup water
Directions:
— Clean and scale fish. Make three crosswise slashes on each side.
— Place fish on a plate and sprinkle with wine, salt, and ginger juice.
— Place plate in steamer and steam for fifteen minutes.
— Heat two tbsp oil and fry green pepper, red pepper, ginger, and cucumber pickle. Add vinegar, sugar, soy sauce, and sesame oil.
— Mix cornstarch with water, add to sauce mixture, bring to boil.
— Cover fish with sauce and serve hot.

"There, you see," announced John, "Ana remembered. If some old computer can remember, so can you," John encouraged. "Ana, can you simulate all the ingredients besides the fish, which will be replaced by the groundcover?"

"Certainly," replied Ana.

"Xia, can you cook up all this if Ana helps?" Xia looked nervously at John and again shook her head no. "Will you at least try?" John coaxed, "Will you try for me? I'd like to taste it, and I'm sure all of our friends would too."

Xia lowered her head but raised her eyes to meet his. She looked at him intensely for a few seconds. John thought he saw a flash of light in them, and then she shook her head yes ever so slightly.

"Done!" John exclaimed, grabbing her hand, pulling her out onto the floor, and dancing around the room. "Sweet and sour groundcover it will be!"

John and Xia spent the entire next day huddled together in a separate section of the food-preparation area. Some of the other colonists were there too, and everyone made sure they not only maintained the utmost secrecy during their food preparation but respected the privacy of each other also. John even had an idea of a quick recipe he could prepare and enter into the contest himself.

When time came for third mess, everyone was ready, and their covered dishes were lining the table in the front of the mess hall. Each dish was covered with the same, domed lid so no one could tell who the preparer of which dish was. Wan then started the evening off with a brief introduction.

"Welcome! Tonight, we're having the 'Groundcover Recipe Challenge,' and I've arranged with the captain for a special surprise." The captain nodded, and everyone in the room gave their complete attention to Wan's next announcement. "When I suggested this a couple weeks ago, Malcolm asked what the prize was," everyone laughed, remembering Malcolm's sarcastic suggestion. "The captain has agreed that the winner of tonight's challenge will have the privilege of giving the groundcover an official name." This brought a universal round of approval from the assembly, including some sporadic clapping. "So, with that, let's begin."

Wan moved aside while still addressing the group. "I'd like all of you to come up, take a small helping of each dish, return to your seat and try them out. You can discuss any and all dishes with your tablemates, but please limit your discussions to the taste of the food and try to maintain the anonymity of the dishes. In about fifteen minutes, I'll call for a vote, and the dish with the most votes will win," Wan concluded and motioned to the group to begin sampling the dishes.

There were only five dishes. Not everyone had made one. It didn't take long for all those assembled to take a serving of each, return to their tables and start tasting. The atmosphere in the mess hall was raucous. Praises and jokes came from every corner. The captain and the first officer took part and were obviously pleased with both the quality of the food and the comradery being displayed. The doctor and Lyuba were prominent also, but the minister and his wife were conspicuously absent. No one asked or cared why.

The announced fifteen minutes stretched into twenty and then to thirty. Second helpings of various dishes were commonplace. Finally, Wan stood up, asked for everyone's attention, and pointing to each dish, one-by-one, asked for a show of hands. Many people voted twice or three times, but in the end, the winner was undeniable.

"Okay," Wan finally declared, "we have a winner!" and she moved over to the third dish on the table. Everyone clapped in agreement. "Whose dish is this?" she asked, but no one jumped up to claim it.

After a few awkward seconds, John stood up with a broad smile and suggested, "Why don't we ask Ana? Ana, whose dish is the third dish?"

Ana replied, "The third dish is Xia's."

The room erupted in applause. They all stood in salute to Xia and gave her a long, standing ovation. Xia shyly lowered her head, but John could make out more than just a hint of a smile this time.

After the room quieted down, Wan continued, "So Xia, you've won the right to name Kepler-438b's groundcover."

"Yes, and it's about time too!" Malcolm yelled out from the back. "I'm getting really tired of going around always saying 'groundcover this' and 'groundcover that.' It's getting boring!" Everyone laughed and turned to Xia.

Xia sat in silence. She looked at John, and her eyes asked for help. John immediately spoke up, "Hey! Give her time to think. This is an important event. Let's savor the moment for a while."

The room quieted down. Everyone recognized John's move to take the pressure off Xia. The question was, would she offer a name, or would John have to offer one for her? The room went back to eating. Third and fourth helpings were encouraged. Most made sure to walk by Xia's table on their way back from the front, showing her they had taken more of her dish and complimenting her on it.

John decided he wouldn't try to coax her into coming up with a name tonight. He thought tomorrow would be a better time to revisit the subject. He wasn't even sure she understood what she was being asked to do.

Then John felt Xia tug on his arm. She handed him an e-tablet. On it were the symbols 鱼植物 . He stared in amazement, not even realizing she could write on a tablet, much less write in what appeared to be Chinese. He looked at Xia, and she nodded. This must be the name, he thought.

John stood up and asked for everyone's attention. "Xia's come up with the name, but I can't read it," he happily announced. "Ana, can you tell us what this says?" he said, holding up the tablet.

"Those are the simplified Chinese radicals 'yu', 'zhi,' and 'wu,' " Ana dutifully replied.

"'You-she-woo?" he repeated, "Okay, but what does that mean in English?"

"'Yu' means 'fish,' 'zhi' means 'plant,' and 'wu' means 'thing' or 'creature.' So, a translation into English of 'yuzhiwu' could be 'fish-plant.'

"Fish-plant!" John exclaimed, "Yu-zhi-wu. Yu-zhi-wu." he kept repeating.

"Yu-zhi-wu!" the room picked up the chant. "Yu-zhi-wu! Yu-zhi-wu! Yu-zhi-wu!"

Xia raised her head and broke out into a big smile. She looked up at John and reached out for his hand. John looked into Xia's eyes and saw a happiness he had not seen for a long, long time.

"At least I can take pride that my 'yuzhiwu on the barbie' came in second!" crowed Malcolm.

"No way," protested Gagandeep, "I'm sure the 'yuzhiwu tikka masala' got the second-most votes."

"What about my 'tom yum yuzhiwu'?" Wan asked, "It got a lot of votes too!"

"Well, I'm pretty sure my 'yuzhiwu burgers' didn't go

over that well, "John jokingly complained. "There's still a lot of them left!"

Zawadi stood up and announced, "Well, I think they all were delicious! And I think they all should be kept on our regular menu! Who's for that?" she asked, and everyone roared their approval.

After the room had quieted down, the captain got up and addressed the group. "Before we call it a night, let's go over the domicile assignments. Tomorrow, you should all move into your permanent quarters in the dome. We need you to clear out of here so Zawadi and Malcolm can put the finishing touches on the compound, and to do that, they need these last structures. She turned to the first officer who handed her his e-tablet with the assignments.

"Although it doesn't really matter which pair gets which double-unit since they're all the same, here's what we've scheduled. If you have other ideas, just let us know. Wan and Gagandeep will be in Unit 1A. It's in the front and nearest the greenhouse. Malcolm and Zawadi will be in Unit 1B. John and Xia will be in Unit 1C. It's at the back and nearest the laboratory and the zygotes." She paused and glanced up at the group, "Any questions?"

The colonists looked at each other and then to Zawadi. On cue, Zawadi stood up and announced, "We've been talking, and would like to suggest some changes to those arrangements."

The captain looked a little surprised, "Go on," she acknowledged.

"Hoke and I would like to share quarters," she began.

"That's right," confirmed Hoke.

"So, we could share Unit 1B," the captain looked down at the first officer for help, "or, if you'd prefer, we could share Hoke's unit on the second floor, Unit 2C."

"If you took Unit 1B, where would Malcolm live?"

countered the captain.

Malcolm then stood up and went over to sit down beside Gagandeep, "I would share a room with Gagandeep. That's what we want to do anyway," he announced, taking Gagandeep's hand that lay on top of the table.

"And I could either live in Unit 1A or Unit 1B," Wan volunteered, "whichever one was available. It doesn't matter to me."

The captain stood speechless. She finally did look at John. "Unit C's fine for Xia and me," he quickly assured her.

The captain and the first officer huddled together for a moment. Then the captain said, "Well, any of those arrangements are okay with us, I guess. Just work it out among yourselves and let us know," she acquiesced, "Just be sure you're all moved in there and out of here by end-of-day tomorrow."

With that, the captain and crew, except for Hoke, exited the mess hall leaving the colonists to themselves.

"All in all, I think this was a very successful night," observed Malcolm.

"Yes," several others chimed in.

"A very successful night indeed," echoed John while smiling at Xia and patting her hand.

Chapter 9

Harbingers

After the colonists and crew relocated to their permanent quarters in the dome, the days started to settle down into more of a routine. Zawadi had moved into Hoke's unit on the second level. After discussions with the captain and first officer, it was decided it was important to have Hoke there with the rest of the crew. Malcolm and Gagandeep were sharing Unit 1A on the first floor, and Wan had Unit 1B all to herself. John and Xia shared Unit 1C as planned and were doing well.

Xia had recovered a little more of her abilities to take care of herself. She routinely dressed, showered, and fed herself, but her speech remained completely absent. Her ability to perform her duties as guardian based on the special skill set required, however, was degraded to the point that Lyuba was drafted to help John in the lab. Xia would accompany them and assist them where she was able, but the brunt of the planning and work was done by John and Lyuba. Both John and Lyuba thought Xia would be able to assist them at a later stage in the operation when she could focus her efforts on caring for the infants and toddlers.

Zawadi and Malcolm's duties, having completed the construction of the major components of the compound, now turned to fine-tuning and maintenance. They, along with Hoke, were constantly reviewing and revising the settings on the nuclear pile so it would produce adequate energy with the most efficiency. They did have a good system of storage for excess energy, enough to last the colony for many months, but its capacity was not infinite. Once it was full, any additional excess energy would have to be dissipated into the atmosphere as heat. At this time, that was not seen to be a big problem, but over a longer period, the introduction of even small amounts of excess heat into Kepler-438b's atmosphere could have unexpected and undesirable results. The fewer changes introduced at this point, until more was known about Kepler-438b's strange, seemingly uniform ecosystem, the better.

Wan and Gagandeep had excelled at populating their greenhouse with an impressive variety of edible, Earth plants. They had successfully sprouted beans, tomatoes, lettuce, cabbage, and carrots, and had even been able to coax several varieties of fruit trees into small saplings. The biggest challenge they had was the lack of soil. Ilithya-2 had brought a modest quantity of potting soil, and Wan and Gagandeep had devised a method of collecting leftover food and delivering it to a composting area. Still, as the colony grew, this lack of native soil could eventually become a big problem.

The minister and his wife were seldom seen. They preferred to cloister themselves in their large living area on the third level of the dome. Zawadi and Malcolm were the only ones who had actually been up there, and then not since the minister had moved in. It was rumored to be extravagantly furnished with many artifacts the minister had brought from Earth, but their only visitors seemed to be the doctor and occasionally the captain.

About once a week, the minister and his wife would

join everyone for second mess. They would eat with the captain, first officer, and the doctor, and only afterward would take a carefully choreographed walk, always accompanied by the doctor, among the other crew and colonists. There were smiles, special acknowledgments of some of the teams' accomplishments, and even some small talk exchanged, but for the most part, it was little more than a dutiful "fly-by."

"What are their names?" John asked once after the minister had retired from the mess hall.

"The minister's name is Majud Hashim," Zawadi responded. "I remember that from when he was first introduced. His wife's name is Jana or Janan, something like that."

"Ana, what is the minister's wife's given name?" John inquired.

"The minister's wife's given name is Janan, but you are to address them as 'Minister' or 'My Lord,' and 'My Lady,' " Ana advised.

"Ha! Fat chance of that!" Malcolm loudly huffed.

The group, as it turned out, got their chance to get "up close and personal" with the minister and his wife the very next day. In the morning at first mess, the doctor announced that the minister would be touring all the areas to see firsthand the progress that each team had been making. Tomorrow would be the zygote lab, the second day would be the control center, and the third and last day would be the greenhouse. The minister expected all the colonists to be present at each tour. There was some grumbling, but curiosity overcame any reservations, and all agreed to attend. In fact, all were eager, in their own way, to attend. Xia was even excited.

When the appointed time came, everyone had gathered in the zygote lab. John and Lyuba took the lead and showed the minister and his wife around the lab. They made sure they included Xia, although she was very excited, and they kept her mainly in the background. At one point, the minister asked the doctor what Xia's role was. The doctor hemmed and hawed a little and promptly passed the question off to John.

"Xia's going to head the nursery and toddler areas. She's the one who developed our initial plan to start with only four zygotes to determine what, if any, variance will occur in the zygote-to-fetus cycle in this environment." The minister seemed mildly impressed. "She also came up with the winning dish in the *yuzhiwu* recipe contest, and in fact, named the plant herself," he went on while smiling at Xia, who was understandably embarrassed.

"Was that the sweet and sour *yuzhiwu*?" the minister's wife asked.

"Yes," confirmed John, "Yes, it was."

"That's my favorite!" she asserted, "and yours too, isn't it dear?" she added, looking at her husband. The minister just grunted and walked on to the next table.

"When can we expect to have the first births?" he asked, trying to move on from the recipe subject.

"Theoretically, in about eight months, of course," Lyuba responded. "But as Xia previously pointed out, there might be some variances due to local conditions, like the Kepler-438b's circadian cycle, or its orbital timeline, or even the electromagnetic fields native to the planet. We just don't know for sure, and that's why Xia suggested an abbreviated first cycle."

This tour ended with the minister shaking all three of the guardians' hands, congratulating them on their progress, and taking his leave. As they were leaving, the doctor turned and smiled at John, Lyuba, and Xia, and gave them a "thumbs up" on a job well done.

The next day right after first mess, they were all to meet in the control room. During first mess, however, the doctor revealed a change in plans. He announced because of the control room's limited size, not all colonists could attend the minister's tour. He suggested that only Zawadi, Malcolm, and Hoke be present during the minister's inspection. He, the doctor, would accompany him, of course, but the minister's wife would not come on this tour either. This news was fine with everyone and, in fact, well-received. Later, Zawadi, Malcolm, and Hoke told everyone about the tour, but it was uneventful. In fact, the minister suggested Zawadi, seemed bored.

The next day, all assembled in the greenhouse. This time, the full complement was there, including all the colonists, the captain, first officer, Hoke, and Lyuba. When the doctor brought the minister and his wife in, the captain and all the crew, excepting Hoke, gave a little bow of their heads. As the minister walked past the colonists, some of the colonists did also, more out of reflex than actual respect. Xia giggled and welcomed the pair with a full, deep bow. John jerked her hand and rolled his eyes but said nothing.

The doctor called for Wan and Gagandeep to walk with them and guide the minister through their handiwork. They nervously complied, and the colonists were not surprised to hear them address the pair as "My Lord" and "My Lady." Malcolm, however, was disgusted, and Zawadi had to hiss him into restraint.

The tour was going well. The minister's wife was especially chatty, talking with Wan while they walked as if they were old friends. They had gone down one row, reached the end, and turned around to return when halfway back, she stopped to especially admire the tomato patch. They were far enough along to be sprouting small, green buds, which would eventually turn into luscious, red tomatoes, or so Wan told her. While examining them, the minister's wife noticed several cracks in the windows.

"What are these?" she asked innocently.

Wan leaned over to examine the cracks, "I don't know, My Lady. I've never noticed them before," she responded.

"I cleaned all these windows just two days ago, and I saw no cracks then," Gagandeep chimed in while moving over to examine the cracks.

"Look!" exclaimed the minister's wife, "Here are some more."

"Where?" asked Wan in disbelief.

"Here," gestured the minister's wife, "and there also," she said as she pointed to more cracks in windowpanes farther down the row.

Wan and Gagandeep just stared at each other in silence. The minister gave the doctor a disapproving look, then turned to Wan and Gagandeep, switched to a smile, and said, "Thank you so much for your tour. Keep up the good work." He then gathered up his wife and walked towards the back of the greenhouse and the entrance to the dome. When there, they both turned around, smiled, and waved to all assembled. Then they were gone.

As soon as they had left, Zawadi and Malcolm rushed over to examine the cracks. "There are cracks!" Zawadi exclaimed, "...and lots of them. Look here, and here, and over there!"

"Could it be the fault of the floating foundations?" Malcolm offered. "Maybe they're flexing more than we anticipated causing a twist on the window frames."

"No," countered Zawadi, "I don't think so, but that's a possibility we'll have to investigate."

"Well, whatever it is, I want it fixed!" barked the doctor, "And I want it fixed quickly! It was an embarrassment for the minister and his wife to be the ones to discover this."

"I, for one, am glad they did discover this," responded Malcolm, "At least they seem to be good for something."

The doctor frowned ominously at Malcolm, "I'd watch your tongue if I were you," he warned.

"Why? What's the minister going to do? Have me exiled to a distant planet?" he spat back.

"Of course not!" replied the doctor, "But he is the minister, you know. He's not someone to trifle with."

Malcolm and the doctor ended their verbal jousting with a stare-down. The doctor finally backed off and walked out of the greenhouse in a huff.

Xia squeezed John's hand and looked at him quizzically.

"It's nothing," John replied, "Just a spat. It has nothing to do with you," he reassured her, but he thought it might be something he'd have to keep an eye on.

Replacing the cracked windowpanes was not a problem. Zawadi and Malcolm had a fairly generous supply of windowpanes and were able to install them in just an hour or so. They were most anxious to discover just why the cracks appeared. There was nothing apparent around the windows or the visible wall, either inside or out. They decided they'd have to move the seedbeds from the wall to investigate further. When they did, they discovered something very troubling.

There were small, reddish tendrils protruding through the joint between the wall and the floor. This joint was a tightly sealed joint having been sealed on Earth. The entire greenhouse had been part of one of the levels of Ilithya-2, and this joint had maintained its integrity throughout the entire voyage. A quick spot-check on other areas, including both sides, showed similar, tendril breaches.

Zawadi and Malcolm immediately set out to disable the tendrils. They first went around the exterior of the entire greenhouse and cut the tendrils at their source with a laser. They wore protective headgear and breathing apparatus that was now mandated as standard equipment when lasering the groundcover to provide protection from the noxious vapors. They also used the laser to burn a strip fifty centimeters wide around the entire structure as a barrier to encroaching groundcover. Inside, they exposed all the walls and used hand-held lasers to burn off the intruding tendrils. This took them two days.

After all that was complete, they began an examination of all the other structures. Unfortunately, they found similar conditions. The groundcover, now known as "*yuzhiwu*," had been able to penetrate most of the structures through the sealed joints. A thorough inspection of the containment structure around the nuclear pile, generators, and control area was more promising. The fifty-centimeter polymer wall, being poured, was jointless, and there was no evidence of any breaches. Zawadi and Malcolm applied the same remedies to this structure anyway and hoped that would be sufficient. After a week and many more inspections of all the buildings, this solution seemed to be working. No more tendrils appeared in the joints.

The civil-engineering pair made up a schedule for lasering back the encroaching *yuzhiwu*. It kept them busy and cut into some of their time they'd planned to use for system optimizations and other maintenance, but everyone recognized the importance of this new task.

This reprieve lasted less than two weeks.

One morning after first mess and after the colonists had dispersed to their separate areas and jobs, Gagandeep came running down the stairs into the Sub-Level 1 control room shouting for Zawadi and Malcolm, "Come quick!" he implored, "Wan's just found some tendrils that have come through the floor. No joints there, just the solid floor!"

Zawadi and Malcolm quickly accompanied Gagandeep to the greenhouse, where Wan was down on her hands and knees crawling along the floor. "They're everywhere!" she wailed, "Everywhere! What can we do?"

Zawadi and Malcolm also got down on their hands and knees to examine the floor. Wan was right. Small, pink, delicate-looking *yuzhiwu* tendrils could be found everywhere peeking up out of the solid floor. They were only several millimeters long, but their presence was unmistakable and very troubling.

"When did you first notice these?" Malcolm asked.

"Just now!" Wan replied with panic in her voice, "Just now!"

"So, you saw nothing like this, nothing to even indicate something amiss, yesterday?"

"No, I swear!" confirmed Wan, "And I sweep the floors every day. Sometimes twice a day if we're doing any pruning. This morning is the first I've seen anything like this."

Zawadi and Malcolm marked off the greenhouse floor into four uneven sections. In the largest section which took up full three-quarters of the greenhouse, they would burn the tendrils back with a laser as they did before. This would at least allow Wan and Gagandeep to continue to care for their plants. In two other, much smaller sections, they would apply two yet-to-be-determined substances: one would be an acid that would dissolve the tendrils, and one would be a poison that would kill the tendrils. They'd use the fourth smaller section as a "control group." Here they would do nothing; just let the tendrils grow to measure their speed and effect on the structure.

They brought in their equipment that morning and had the major section lasered clean before second mess. After eating, they commandeered the medical lab and enlisted, drafted really, the help of Gagandeep, John, Lyuba, and even the doctor to run some tests to determine the best corrosive and poisonous solutions to apply to the tendrils. John and Lyuba were tasked with coming up with a corrosive, and Gagandeep and the doctor with an effective poison. Xia, of course, tagged along and made herself useful preparing testing surfaces and cleaning up. By the end of the day, they had tested over twenty off-the-shelf substances, and both pairs had good candidates for the job.

John and Lyuba, with Xia's assistance, settled on a microbial corrosive featuring a chemoautotroph that attacked organic materials but not inorganic ones. They thought this would confine the corrosion to the *yuzhiwu* tendrils while sparing the building components. Gagandeep and the doctor, having already done many experiments on the *yuzhiwu* to determine the nutritional value, settled on a synthetic allelopath that mimicked the natural, hormonal-based herbicide produced by an Earth walnut. This solution seemed to be especially effective on *yuzhiwu*. Armed with these two substances, Zawadi and Malcolm began their eradication efforts the first thing the next morning.

The microbial corrosive worked the fastest. Within an hour, the tendrils had started to darken, become stiff, and were apparently dying. By the end of the day, all the tendrils treated with the powerful corrosive had turned completely black, become brittle, and were easily swept away. Closer examination, including some very shallow excavation into the floor, showed the same results for the portions of the tendrils below the surface.

The synthetic allelopath took longer. There were some minor changes to the tendrils by day's end, but nothing dramatic was observed until the morning of the third day. Then, the tendrils quickly turned black, brittle, and like those treated with the microbial corrosive, died and were easily swept up. Excavation of the floor in this section also showed the effects extended well below the floor's surface.

Now, these sections would be left alone to see which treatment proved to be the longest-lasting.

In the "control section" the tendrils grew about five millimeters a day, or half a centimeter. This was the same rate as observed in *yuzhiwu* growing out on the planet's surface. This growth rate continued for two days until this section was further divided into two sections, and each treated with either the microbial corrosive or the synthetic allelopath with the same successful results.

Zawadi and Malcolm checked all the other structures for similar incursions and did find several. They treated these with one or the other of the two substances and then could only wait. The work in the lab, however, did not stop. Other corrosives and herbicides were tested. Some proved effective, but none appreciably more so than the two already recommended.

The tendrils reappeared in the section treated with the microbial corrosive five days later. They were immediately treated with the synthetic allelopath, but it seemed to have no effect on them. They continued to maintain their healthy, pinkish color and grew at a steady rate of five millimeters a day. If this wasn't alarming enough, tendrils appeared two days later in the section that had originally been treated with the synthetic allelopath. They were subjected to a treatment of the microbial corrosive, but again, there was no effect. Zawadi and Malcolm eradicated the tendrils in both sections with lasers, and the lab technicians redoubled their efforts to find a more effective treatment.

Over the next several weeks, many new solutions were developed, tested, and applied. The results were all the same, both in the lab and in the field. The treatments would all have varying initial success in killing *yuzhiwu* tendrils, but, when they grew back, and they always did, the substances would have little or no effect. This was a universal phenomenon. If they treated tendrils in the greenhouse, new tendrils in the dome would very quickly display the same resistance to the corrosive or poisonous substances. This, of course, lent more weight to the growing theory that all *yuzhiwu* was not only the same kind of organism but, in fact, all the very same organism. It appeared that the entire surface of Kepler-438b was covered by one and only one living being – *yuzhiwu*.

Zawadi and Malcolm started looking for other solutions to this growing and very disturbing problem. One of the most promising was to resituate all the building onto columns or stilts. These stilts would elevate the building to a height above the *yuzhiwu* so any creeping tendrils could be lasered before they reached the floors or walls. The stilts themselves could either be made of a truly impervious material, like the polymer that was used to line the nuclear pile's containment area. This area had not yet shown any signs of a breach by *yuzhiwu*; or the stilts could be constructed so they could be easily replaced, maybe made so they were disposable and could be swapped out in place with new stilts. While all these alternatives were developed, analyzed, and presented to the captain, which in turn were presumably discussed with the minister, the only course of action that could be taken now was the constant and regular lasering of encroaching tendrils.

With all attempts meeting with failure and new suggestions seemingly mired down in either a clash of, or absence of, leadership, the colonists felt like they were spending every day just trying to keep their heads above water and fighting for their very lives.

It was in this chaotic arena that Gagandeep brought Malcolm into the hospital to see the doctor.

Chapter 10

Infestation

The jungle was unusually alive tonight. John again lay by the stream, gazing into the lazily moving waters. The underbrush behind him was rustling with life. He rolled over quickly and peered into the darkness. The noises stopped, but as soon as he turned back to the stream, they started up again. The canopy over his head also seemed to be moving, but when he'd look, he could discern nothing. He felt very uneasy and unwelcome, as if he was an intruder. John slept fitfully all night and woke unsettled.

* * * *

"So, what brings you here?" asked the doctor with mild irritation looking up from his e-tablet as Gagandeep and Malcolm stood in his doorway.

"It's just a cough," replied Malcolm defensively. "I told Gagandeep, it was nothing, but he insisted I come see you."

"Just a cough, huh?" the doctor repeated disinterestedly. "How long have you had it?"

"He's been coughing, especially in the mornings, for almost a week now," volunteered Gagandeep. "It's getting worse. That's why I suggested he come see you."

"Okay, peel down your coveralls and let me listen to your chest," said the doctor as he dug out his computer-assisted stethoscope. "Now just breathe normally," he continued as he moved the stethoscope around Malcolm's chest and then to his back. The doctor turned to the computer readout and confirmed that there was nothing abnormal in Malcolm's stethoscope readings. "Open up and say 'aah,' " the doctor ordered and proceeded to peer down Malcolm's throat. "Looks like a mild case of xerostomia to me." Malcolm frowned. "Dry throat," translated the doctor. "That can be caused by low humidity, but I doubt that's the case on this planet. How about your air-conditioner? Do you run it often, like when sleeping?"

"No," Gagandeep interjected, "We don't find a need for air-conditioning much. Maybe sometime during the day if we're in our unit, but never at night."

"Have you been taking in plenty of fluids?" the doctor continued his questioning.

"Yes," responded Malcolm, "At least as much as usual. There's been no change in my habits there."

"How about work? Do you work outside a lot?"

"Not so much now as we used to. Zawadi and I spend most of our time lasering down all those stinking weeds," Malcolm replied disgustedly. "Maybe it's the smoke from the *yuzhiwu*," he offered.

"Are you wearing your protective masks and breathing-assist canisters?" asked the doctor.

"Sure!" assured Malcolm. "I saw what those fumes did to John and Xia. Zawadi and I are very conscientious about that. We even have a routine to check each other's gear before we start lasering," he added.

"Good," acknowledged the doctor. "In that case, I recommend you gargle with salt water a couple times a day."

"Saltwater? That doesn't sound like it would help a sore throat," protested Malcolm.

"Yes, I know it sounds counter-intuitive, but it's a tried-and-true method of treating a dry, sore throat. Give it a try for a few days. If it doesn't help, come back and see me," he advised. With that, Malcolm and Gagandeep left, and the doctor went back to his research on his e-tablet. His time now was virtually totally consumed with trying to find an effective herbicide or pesticide, or some combination thereof, to deal with the problematic *yuzhiwu*.

Over the next several days, Zawadi and Malcolm, in fact, the entire community, concentrated most of their efforts on either dealing directly with the continuing encroachment of the persistent *yuzhiwu*, or thinking about ways to stop, manage, or mitigate its potentially destructive incursions. Hoke was one of the most concerned and made daily checks on the walls and floors of the nuclear pile's containment area. So far, however, the very durable polymer seemed to be holding its own against *yuzhiwu*'s continuing structural assaults.

* * * *

Several days later, Gagandeep awoke to Malcolm coughing violently and saw blood smears on his pillow. They immediately had Ana arouse the doctor and rushed to the hospital area.

After a short physical examination of Malcolm's throat, the doctor reported, "Nothing here. The blood isn't coming from the throat. I'd better take a closer look," he suggested. "Let's go in the other room, and we'll take a look at you with the MRI unit."

Malcolm pulled up his coveralls, and all three started across the hall. "You should wait out here," the doctor advised Gagandeep at the door, "I don't want to unnecessarily expose you to the magnetic field. I'll be wearing a protective face shield and apron, but I only have one set." Gagandeep reluctantly waited outside.

The doctor instructed Malcolm to remove his coveralls and lie down on the table of the MRI unit. While he was doing that, the doctor turned on the MRI unit and adjusted the settings. "You have to lie very still while the MRI is scanning," commanded the doctor, "It won't take long, but it is pretty loud, so don't let that startle you."

With the doctor's help, Malcolm situated himself on the table. The doctor disappeared behind his shield, and the table retracted into the MRI unit. The target was Malcolm's chest area. Just as the doctor advised, the scanning didn't take long, but it certainly was loud. When the scans were complete, the table moved back out of the scanning unit, and the doctor helped Malcolm up. As Malcolm was dressing, the doctor went into the room next door to pull up the results on the computer.

"Ana, please display Malcolm's MRI," the doctor requested. The results were very puzzling. His lungs seemed generally clear, there was no fluid, but there were several fine, fibrous growths that seemed to emanate from within the inferior ventral portion of his left lung and wind downwards into his pleural cavity. He had Ana slowly rotate the MRI hologram on a vertical axis and discovered more of the same fibers emanating from within the inferior dorsal portion of his right lung. These fibers appeared to be very fine and about fifteen centimeters in length. The first two or three centimeters appeared to originate within the lung, then extend through the lung wall into the pleural cavity, and finally wind downwards for ten to twelve centimeters.

There was no doubt in the doctor's mind that these fibers were causing Malcolm's cough and bloody expectorant. What he didn't know was what they were.

They could be some kind of abnormal cellular growths, they could be benign or malignant, or even some kind of parasite. To make an exact determination, he would have to extract a specimen. That would be tricky. He'd either have to do that by inserting an instrument down into Malcolm's lung through his mouth and throat or go in through his lower abdomen. Either way, would require a general anesthetic. He thought he'd better give this more thought and research it with Ana before making a decision on a procedure.

"What did you find, doc?" Malcolm asked as he entered the room accompanied by Gagandeep. The doctor immediately dismissed the hologram and turned to address them.

"Nothing much," he began, "There is some evidence of some foreign substance in your lungs, but I can't tell what it is. I don't think it's anything to worry about. Probably something you've inhaled while working outside, or when incinerating the *yuzhiwu*."

"I do plenty of that," agreed Malcolm.

"Let me do some quick research with Ana, and I'll get back to you this afternoon with a recommendation."

"Okay, doc," Malcolm agreed, "Thanks."

"Yes, thanks a lot," added Gagandeep as they left.

As soon as they'd disappeared down the corridor, the doctor sat back down at his desk, "Ana, please cross-reference Malcolm's MRI with your medical database to find matches. Let me know as soon as you find anything."

"Yes, doctor," Ana acknowledged.

Later that morning at first mess, the doctor made a point of circulating around the various tables and mingling with all the colonists. He started with sitting and eating with the captain and first officer, then moved to sit a bit with John, Xia, Lyuba, and Wan. He only stopped briefly to say hi to Malcolm and Gagandeep, asking how Malcolm was doing and receiving an encouraging "better" reply. Just as they were getting up to leave, he cornered Zawadi and Hoke and made up some questions about some phantom electrical surges he claimed he had noticed.

"No," replied Zawadi, "We've noticed nothing. In fact, I'm sure I've seen no surges on the daily reports."

"How about you?" the doctor asked directly to Hoke, "Have you noticed any surges?"

Hoke cleared his throat and then replied, "Nope, I've noticed nothing either." After he'd spoken, he turned his head and coughed quietly.

"How long have you had that cough?" the doctor immediately inquired.

"Cough? Oh, that?" he coughed again, "It's nothing. It just started a day or so ago. It'll be gone soon, I'm sure," Hoke assured the doctor.

"I'd like you to come by my office tomorrow morning. I want to check out that cough," the doctor replied.

"It's nothing, doc," Hoke protested, "I get things like this all the time."

"Still, I want you to come in to see me tomorrow morning. It won't take long. I want to run some tests on you."

"It's really not necessary..." Hoke began to protest.

"That's an order," the doctor interrupted. "I have my reasons," he added, looking at Zawadi.

"Yes," interjected Zawadi, "I think that's a good idea. You've had that cough for a few days now. Just go in and have it checked out," she agreed.

Seeing he was outnumbered, Hoke just shrugged his shoulders in resignation and shook his head yes, "What time?"

"Let's make if for right after first mess, about 08:30, okay?"

"Okay," confirmed Hoke as he and Zawadi left the mess hall.

Ana's research turned up nothing that seemed to approximate the fibrous growths emanating from Malcolm's lungs. After some more research, the doctor decided the least invasive way to extract a sample of the growths would be with thoracoscopic surgery. He planned to use a telescopic rod-and-lens system connected to a video camera with a fiber-optic-cable system connected to a "cold," xenon-light source to illuminate the operative field. This gear would be inserted through a 5-millimeter incision. An electrosurgical device would be used to sever sections of the fibrous growths, and a forceps extension would be used to retrieve and extract them.

He had Ana arrange for all the equipment and scheduled the procedure with Malcolm for the next afternoon since the morning would be taken up with Hoke's MRI.

The next morning right after first mess, Hoke and Zawadi showed up at the hospital area for Hoke's MRI. Of course, Hoke didn't know he was to have an MRI until after he went through the normal, preliminary physical and the computer-assisted examination. The doctor, having found no other signs which could account for Hoke's cough, suggested the MRI.

"MRI? No way!" protested Hoke. "An MRI for just a cough? Are you crazy?"

The doctor looked at Zawadi for help and did get some support, "I'm sure the doctor has his reasons," interjected Zawadi. "And besides, I want you to take advantage of every precaution available. We're not living on Earth where everything is familiar and routine," she reminded him. "Best get this checked out before it becomes something big."

Hoke, of course, finally relented and followed the doctor into the MRI room. He lay down on the table and was given all the requisite instructions and warnings. When the procedure was completed, the doctor told them to go on about their daily routine, and he would call them when he had the results.

The results, of course, were immediately available. As soon as they left, he prompted Ana to display them and, unfortunately, found exactly what he was looking for: fibrous growths similar to Malcolm's. There weren't as many, and they weren't as long, but they were unmistakably present. The doctor pondered the situation for only a short time and then began to prepare the room, his equipment, and himself for the procedure on Malcolm scheduled for this afternoon.

During his preparations, he decided he needed an assistant, or at least he thought an assistant would be prudent. He immediately thought of Wan. She had been handy around the lab when they were doing the early experimentation on *yuzhiwu*. He had Ana contact her and drafted her into service for that afternoon. He told her they could meet for second mess, and he would explain more about the procedure itself and what would be expected of her. That briefing went well, and right after second mess, they returned to the hospital area where the doctor familiarized Wan with the equipment, and then, they waited for Malcolm.

Before Gagandeep and Malcolm showed up, the doctor had decided against a general anesthetic. It was too dangerous, especially without skilled assistance, and by choosing a thoracoscopic procedure, he would only need to apply a mild sedative and a topical anesthetic. But before any of that, he wanted to do another MRI. It had been a day and a half now since the first MRI, Malcolm was decidedly worse, and he'd like to know if and how things had changed.

Malcolm's new MRI showed the fibrous growths had increased in length, girth, and even in number. The doctor did not share this information with anyone, even Wan. It wouldn't make any difference. The next thing to be done now was the extraction of specimens. After that, he would, well.., he wasn't really sure what he would do after that. First things first.

He made some notes, and using the MRI image, selected two of the growths that were close together. Once inside, he would make a laser incision on one short growth close to the lung wall, extract it, and then, if that was successful, would go back in and clip a portion off a longer growth in another location. The doctor wanted to get as many samples as he could so he could parse them out over a variety of still-undefined experiments.

The doctor administered the sedative, applied the topical anesthetic, then he and Wan occupied Malcolm with small talk for about fifteen minutes until he seemed to relax and was not responding to pinpricks around the chosen incision site. Just before starting, the doctor talked him through the procedure.

"First, I'll make a small incision here," he said while smearing antiseptic over the chosen area. Then, I'll enter your chest with this instrument," he continued while holding up the telescopic rod, "locate the foreign matter, and then extract it with this," he pointed to the telescopic forceps. "I might have to do this several times, but you should feel nothing. If you do, let me know immediately."

Malcolm nodded his understanding but said nothing.

"Wan will be monitoring all the systems and will assure you are comfortable," the doctor said, and Wan nodded her head in agreement.

"And I'll be right here too," added Gagandeep, who had scrubbed up and was clothed in a surgical mask and gown. He stood at the side of the bed out of the way and held Malcolm's hand.

"Are you ready?" he asked Malcolm. After getting no reply, not even a nod, he said, "Here we go," and made the initial incision.

The doctor's style was to deliver a constant monolog while performing this type of surgery. He thought it helped keep the patient relaxed. "I'm inserting the video-camera now. I see the image on the screen here. And yes! There's one of the foreign objects. That was easy," he continued on, "Now the clipping of the object. Good. No problem. Now the forceps..., and now out. There!" he proudly announced, "We have one extracted already!" He placed it in a beaker of dilute, saline solution sitting on a tray next to the bed. He would normally place samples in a beaker of alcohol, but he wasn't intending on preserving these specimens, at least not right now. He was interested only in keeping them in as close to the same environment as they were growing inside Malcolm's chest cavity as possible. He repeated the procedure and extracted another, larger specimen.

"Okay, we're finished," he announced as he placed the second specimen in a second beaker. "All I have to do now is sew and seal you up. Easy-peasy!" he added, trying to keep the situation light.

After a few sutures, more antiseptic, and a tight, adhesive seal, he pronounced Malcolm good-to-go. "Take at easy, at least through tomorrow. No strenuous work," he warned, "and don't shower before you come back and see me in two days," he advised, "Damp-cloth baths only!"

"We'll be careful," Gagandeep promised. With that, Malcolm dressed, and the two left.

"What now?" asked Wan.

"Now, we examine the specimens," the doctor replied. "In fact, you can get started. Take them into the lab, take some scrapings from each, and set them up so Ana can run DNA tests on them. That's what I want to see first," the doctor ordered. "Set them up in the same manner as we set up the tests on the groundcover. And tell Ana to contact me when she has the results."

"Will do," Wan acknowledged, and with that, she took the two beakers of specimens down the hall, through the dome, and into the lab area on the other side.

The doctor retired to his office to await the results. He busied himself going over more data on possible herbicides and pesticides, but he was just biding time until Wan and Ana had finished their testing. He didn't have to wait long.

"Doctor," announced Ana, "I have the DNA results for the two specimens extracted from Malcolm's chest cavity."

"Display them please," he ordered matter-of-factly. Ana displayed a holographic chart showing the DNA helix of the two specimens side-by-side. "They look the same to me," the doctor observed, "What's your assessment?"

"The DNA in the two specimens are identical," Ana confirmed.

"Now display this DNA with the DNA of *yuzhiwu* we found during the nutritional testing." Another helix appeared in the hologram, "and give me a statistical comparison," he added.

"The DNA of the specimens and the DNA of the groundcover now called *yuzhiwu* are the same within only a slight statistical variation," Ana reported.

"What is the variation?" asked the doctor.

"The DNA in these new samples have a slightly higher ratio of the new nucleotide you have named "keplerine" than the earlier samples," Ana responded.

"How much of a difference?" the doctor asked.

"In the DNA of the earlier samples, the keplerine comprised 11.223% of the DNA chain. In these specimens, the keplerine comprises 11.593% of the nucleotides in the DNA chain.

The doctor sat back in his chair to think. "Ana, ask Zawadi to bring me a fresh sample of *yuzhiwu*. Just a small piece is fine, as long as it's been freshly cut."

"Yes," Ana acknowledged.

In less than ten minutes, Zawadi appeared at his door with a fresh cutting. "Give that to Wan and tell her to prepare it and have Ana run a DNA test on it," ordered the doctor.

Zawadi turned and left the room without speaking.

When Ana alerted the doctor that the tests of this new sample had been completed, he braced himself for the results. "Ana, please give me a statistical comparison of these new samples to the specimens removed from Malcolm."

"They are exactly the same," reported Ana. Her words were just what the doctor both expected and feared.

"Exactly the same?" he asked for confirmation, "Down to what decimal place?"

"Exact is exact to twenty decimal places," Ana confirmed, "Do you want me to extend the calculations out further than that?"

"No," the doctor sighed, "No Ana, that won't be

necessary. Thank you, and please protect all this information as "medical classified." I don't want anyone accessing it, especially Malcolm or any of the colonists."

"Yes, doctor," Ana acknowledged.

What to do? What to do? he thought. He knew he needed at least a two-pronged approach. One was to start running tests to develop a treatment to slow down, stop, and hopefully eradicate this *yuzhiwu* infection, or infestation, or whatever it was. The other was to test the other colonists and crew, including himself, to see how rampant this condition was. The former was the most pressing, but after more thought, he believed the two could be done in parallel. He'd need help, of course, people with some lab skills. He knew he could enlist Wan and Gagandeep, and probably John. Maybe even Lyuba could be utilized, although her skills were less lab-focused and more on the computer side. For these types of tasks, however, the two areas were both equally important. Xia certainly had the skills at one time, but no longer. He thought the first order of business was to fully inform the captain of the situation, and then, of course, the minister, although that would have to be handled very delicately.

He asked Ana to schedule a meeting with the captain as soon as possible. He told her to tell the captain it was a very critical medical emergency. This evening would be none too soon. He could be ready in an hour, as soon as he could get the data together and detail out his nascent plans and recommendations. How could she say no?

Right after third mess, the doctor, the captain, and first officer met in one of the offices on the second level of the dome. The meeting didn't last long, and the captain and first officer approved all of the doctor's recommendations and pledged their unqualified support. After the meeting, the doctor met with Wan and briefed her. She was going to have to step up and learn to perform the MRI's by herself, freeing the doctor to his other task – developing a treatment.

At first mess the next morning, the doctor presented a schedule for everyone to come in for a complete checkup, including an MRI. The schedule was for two colonists or crew each morning, and two in the afternoon, for the next two days. That would cover everyone except the doctor and the minister and his wife. He would have Wan give him an MRI when they had the time, and he himself would have to deal with the minister and his wife. There were a lot of questions that arose. He dismissed them all out-of-hand, claiming it was necessary due to a medical emergency. Everyone already knew or had heard rumors, of Malcolm spitting up blood. A few knew about Hoke's visit to the doctor, but no one had made the connection. After some grumbling, however, everyone resigned themselves to complying with the schedule.

The first two were scheduled for that very morning, first Gagandeep and then John. The doctor conducted all checkups the same. First was a quick preparation before the patient arrived where he would browse through their medical history with Ana's help. When they arrived, he would ask some questions about their assessment of their general health, perform a brief, external examination of their pulmonary system, examine their throat, draw blood, and then perform an MRI. He involved Wan in all of this with the goal of handing over the blood work and MRI procedure to her. This would free him up to work with the others, Gagandeep and John, in the lab. This is why he scheduled their checkups first.

After the two morning checkups, Wan said she

thought she could handle the blood work and the MRI with no supervision. The doctor agreed, reminding her he'd be in the lab should she need anything. The rest of the checkups, Lyuba and Xia, Zawadi and the first officer, the captain and Wan, and finally, the doctor himself went off without a hitch. The doctor had arranged for a private check-up time in the evening for the minister and his wife and performed all the procedures for them himself.

While he was waiting on all the MRI's and blood work to come in, he asked Ana to display the definitions for "infection" and "infestation." Ana dutifully displayed a hologram with the following text:

Definitions of Infection and Infestation

Infection: the state produced by the establishment of a pathogen in or on a suitable host
Infestation: the noun form of the verb infest
Infest: to live in or on as a parasite

Although both fit, since *yuzhiwu* straddled the line between plant and animal, the doctor chose to call this condition an infestation.

The work in the lab was now in full swing. The doctor had already decided on two main areas of testing to find an effective treatment for the *yuzhiwu* infestations. They focused on radiation and chemotherapy.

Radiation is usually used when the pathogen is localized, which in the examples he'd seen so far, was the case. They all seem to emanate from the interior wall of the lungs, so their points of origin would be his targets. As long as there were not too many tendrils, he thought radiation would be a good choice.

Chemotherapy is used when the pathogen is dispersed, or even if the affected area is large and spread out. So far, he'd seen no evidence of that, but he wanted to develop treatments using both these general approaches to be ready for anything.

Testing of the radiation treatment would be fairly straightforward. The key would be finding a radiation calibration that combined an effective dosage and duration that would destroy the *yuzhiwu* cells with as little damage as possible to the surrounding lung tissue. The chemotherapy testing was more complex. It not only had to take into account dosages, but the tests also had to include a variety of chemical agents in order to find the best combination.

In the meantime, Malcolm was getting worse. His symptoms, in addition to the cough and bloody sputum, now also included labored breathing, chest pains, and general fatigue. The doctor immediately ordered another MRI and was shocked at the results. The *yuzhiwu* had doubled in size and number and was now not only entwining itself around his lungs but also his heart and spinal cord. The doctor ordered immediate hospitalization and began a treatment with the most promising of the chemotherapy agents. He also ordered Hoke into the hospital and, after another MRI to set targeting parameters, began an aggressive series of radiation treatments on him. Thankfully, both Malcolm's and Hoke's treatments were successful.

After just two chemotherapy treatments, a new MRI showed the tendrils in Malcolm's lungs had been dislodged from his interior lung wall and were apparently dead or dying. Similar results were seen in Hoke. His tendrils began to shrivel up after the first treatment and also appeared to be dead. In both cases, the complete treatment would include one or more thoracoscopic procedures to remove the remnants of the *yuzhiwu* tendrils. The doctor elected to postpone this until and unless it proved necessary, also because he now needed to turn his attention to the potential health issues of other colonists and crew who were, one-by-one, beginning to present symptoms of *yuzhiwu* infestation.

Lyuba now showed the most advanced symptoms, and that was corroborated by her MRI in which her lungs showed the most aggressive spread of *yuzhiwu* tendrils. Because of the early stage of her infestation, the doctor ordered radiation treatments. They also proved to be successful, and the doctor was confident they were turning the corner on this potential catastrophe. After reviewing all the MRI's, including those of the minister and his wife, he ordered chemotherapy treatments on all personnel except two: John and Xia. Their MRI's came back negative. The doctor ordered new MRI's for them but scheduled them as a low priority. In the meantime, the blood work was thoroughly analyzed by Ana, and the results showed trace levels of the newly discovered nucleotide, keplerine, in the red blood cells in all samples except two: John and Xia. This correlation could be nothing. It could just be because John and Xia hadn't yet been infested. The doctor, however, knew it might have more significance and deserved more analysis, but set all that aside for now while he and Wan worked to give all other personnel, including themselves, their scheduled series of chemotherapy treatments. The subsequent MRI's and blood tests confirmed success: dead tendrils and no traces of keplerine in the blood. Now, the colonists and crew turned their attention to the less critical, but still worrisome encroachment, of *yuzhiwu* into their buildings and other structures.

Six days later, Lyuba paid the doctor an early morning visit complaining of a tingling in her left arm. The doctor immediately ordered blood tests and an MRI and discovered the worst. The *yuzhiwu* was back, had reappeared in her lungs, and had already spread to her spinal cord where it was evidently pressing on a ganglion associated with her left arm. The doctor ordered both radiation and chemotherapy treatments, but after a series of four each, both a new MRI and blood tests showed no effect, and, in fact, there was an increase in the infestation.

One-by-one, the colonists and crew succumbed to this new round of infestation, all but two: John and Xia. This fact was now too significant to ignore. The doctor ordered new blood tests from everyone and directed Ana to analyze every molecule, run detailed comparisons to John's and Xia's samples, and report back as soon as possible. In the meantime, all the doctor could do was to try to make his patients as comfortable as possible.

Lyuba was suffering the worst. The numbness in her arm had spread to the entire left side of her body and had then morphed into searing pain. The doctor's only option was to try to mask the excruciating pain with a sedative. He had a supply of dihydromorphinone, a semi-synthetic derivative of morphine. He first confirmed that Ana could synthesize more, then he prescribed dosages for Lyuba. It would be stored in a soft, ingestible capsule and placed directly into the mouth. The patient could bite down on the soft capsule and then swallow the liquid inside. They could then either spit out or ingest the capsule itself. It was fast-acting and very effective at masking pain. It was not long until four patients were confined to hospital beds and receiving this treatment for pain.

Lyuba's condition continued to deteriorate. The doctor considered operating and cutting out all the *yuzhiwu* but finally came to the conclusion that it was just too risky, especially considering that almost certainly the *yuzhiwu* would just return.

His only hope now lies with the analysis of John's and Xia's blood work. Ana had been keeping him informed of her progress, but so far, the only medically significant difference between their blood and the blood of those infested was the absence of the keplerine, but, as the doctor had first considered, there might not be a causal relationship there. The presence of keplerine might only be an effect of the infestation, not a cause. Still, he pressed on.

"Ana, rerun all your tests, and this time look for all molecules or substances that are either both present or both absent in John's and Xia's samples compared to all the other samples," he ordered while rubbing the back of his neck. It had recently started to ache.

"Working...," replied Ana.

The *yuzhiwu* tendrils had penetrated every building in the compound except the containment area encasing the nuclear pile, generators, and control room. Hoke, who was one of the few besides the doctor, John, and Xia, who was now able to get out and function, even if only halfway, checked the walls and floors every day. His worst nightmare was the *yuzhiwu* breaching the outside walls and eventually the inner walls housing the liquid hydrogen causing the pile to overheat, causing a full-blown meltdown releasing large quantities of radioactive waste into the groundcover and the atmosphere. He had set the thresholds for the automatic shutdown very low to try to lessen that risk. Still, it was his worst fear.

Hoke, John, and Xia worked most of the days trying to keep the corridors, especially areas associated with the hospital and its equipment, as clear of *yuzhiwu* as possible. It was a never-ending fight and one which they knew they were slowly losing. *Yuzhiwu* tendrils now covered much of the greenhouse, a large part of floors and walls in the living units and had worked its way up to the second level of the dome. The conditions in the minister's quarters on the third level were known only to the doctor. He reported there was not so much damage there, but that the minister, and especially his wife, were suffering the same as everyone with *yuzhiwu* infestation. The doctor had moved equipment up to their quarters to treat them there and spent a significant amount of time attending to them, much too much time, most of the colonists agreed.

Xia spent a lot of time with Lyuba, having formed a special bond with her after her previous near-death and debilitating encounter with *yuzhiwu*. John spent any personal time he had there with Lyuba also. Her pain was intense. She had capsules of dihydromorphinone beside her bed and used them when necessary. She slept most of the time, but when she was awake and could stand the pain long enough to talk, she very much appreciated Xia's and John's presence.

Xia would start sobbing heavily when she saw Lyuba in so much pain. "Hush now, Xia," scolded John, "Lyuba is going to be fine. The doctor is going to figure this out, and everyone will be fine."

"Have you been sneaking my 'happy juice?' " Lyuba strained to make a joke, "You sound more deluded than me. The doctor has no clue where to go from here. This is

W. D. Smart

not going to end well. I've resigned myself to that," Lyuba said matter-of-factly.

Xia shook her head no and held Lyuba's hand. John nodded his agreement with Xia. "We'll get through this. We'll stick with you. You are our friend."

Later that night when both John and Xia left for a short break, Lyuba made some final arrangements, "Ana," she called out.

"Yes, Lyuba," the ever-present Ana responded.

"If I die," she started, "...when I die," she corrected herself, "you must transfer all my computer clearances to John. Do you understand?"

"Yes," Ana replied, "I understand your order, but that seems to be against regulations. John is a guardian, and as such, can only be given clearances directly associated with his duties."

"Ana, I'm sure even you can see these are not normal circumstances. Rules like that were made for normal circumstances. We're all dying. I order you to grant him my clearances when I die."

"Yes," replied Ana, "I will do that, but why John? Why not the minister, the captain, or the doctor? Why did you choose John?"

"John is my friend, and I trust him," Lyuba replied immediately.

Ana was silent for a moment and then asked, "And although you would not break the rules for yourself, you would for your friend?" Ana questioned, attempting to confirm her fuzzy understanding of the human concept of "friend."

"Yes," replied Lyuba softly, "yes, a friend." Lyuba grimaced slightly as the pain started to return. She ingested another capsule of dihydromorphinone and wearily said to Ana, "That's enough now. I just want to sleep," she added, her words trailing off softly.

"Good night," Ana replied, but there was no response from Lyuba.

As Ana was conversing with Lyuba, she had also contacted the doctor and was advising him of the results of her re-analysis of the blood samples. "What did you find out?" he nervously queried.

"I found many similarities and differences in the various blood samples. After placing them all in a matrix, I finally isolated one component that appears only in John's and Xia's sample, but none of the others."

"What is it?" the doctor asked excitedly.

"An unknown protein," replied Ana.

"Where is the protein located?"

"It is present in their plasma cells."

"You say it's unknown, but what do you think it is?"

"I can only speculate, but it has the same structure as an antibody, an immunoglobulin," Ana replied.

"Immune response!" the doctor excitedly shouted out loud to no one, "An immune response!"

Chapter 11

Immune Response

"So, you say this unknown protein that's unique to John and Xia is possibly an antibody?" the doctor asked of Ana.

"Yes," replied Ana, "that is a possibility."

"Ana, please display the medical definition of 'immune response.' "

Ana immediately displayed the following text:

Definition of Immune Response

Immune Response: a bodily response to an antigen that occurs when lymphocytes identify the antigenic molecule as foreign and induce the formation of antibodies and lymphocytes capable of reacting with it and rendering it harmless.

The doctor looked that over for a few minutes and then requested, "Ana, please display the data." Ana proceeded to display rows and columns of statistical readings until the doctor said, "Stop! Not the raw data.

Summarize it for me, and present it using data visualization."

The rows and columns of data dissolved and were replaced with a chart-like hologram.

Antibodies and Antigens

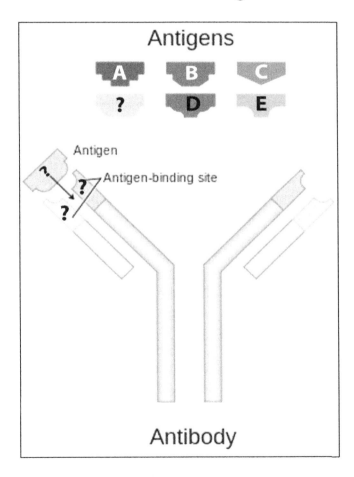

Ana narrated, "As you know, an antibody is a protein that is produced by plasma cells. It is 'L-shaped' and has paratope, sometimes referred to as a 'lock,' that is specific to a unique epitope, sometimes referred to as a 'key,' or specific antigen. When an antibody encounters its matching antigen, it 'locks onto it,' tagging it for attack by the other parts of the immune system.

"Although no humans have exactly the same sets of antibodies, most are present in a majority of humans. After cross-checking all the blood samples, this is the only protein that is shaped like an antibody that is present in only John's and Xia's blood samples."

"Can you identify the antigen it targets?"

"No, not conclusively," Ana admitted, "but anticipating your question, I did run a simulation and came up with a hypothetical antigen whose epitope would match this antibody's paratope."

"And, what did it look like?" asked the doctor.

"The simulated model resembled the newly discovered nucleotide keplerine," Ana responded.

The doctor sat back in his chair. His mind was buzzing. *Could this be the key?*

Xia interrupted him abruptly by barging into his office. Her eyes were wide in fright. She grabbed his arm and started pulling him out of his chair.

The doctor rushed over to check his monitor and saw Lyuba's display flashing red. *Why didn't the alarm sound?* He rushed with Xia to Lyuba's bedside calling for Wan to drop everything and meet him there with a defibrillation unit. It also contained a syringe with adrenaline. As soon as he got to Lyuba, he started performing cardiopulmonary resuscitation but moved to apply the defibrillation procedure as soon as Wan arrived. Nothing worked. Ten minutes later, the doctor pronounced Lyuba deceased, the first victim of the *yuzhiwu* infestation, but she was unfortunately not the last.

Over the next two days, her death was quickly

followed by Malcolm and Hoke. Their deaths were not easy ones. Gagandeep attended Malcolm to the end, as Zawadi did for Hoke. Because of the intense pain, their partners suffered, they kept them heavily sedated with dihydromorphinone, so near the end, there really wasn't much meaningful interaction. In the meantime, the doctor brought John and Xia in and told them he thought the reason they had not been infested was because they had developed immunity when they had their near-death encounters with the *yuzhiwu* vapors.

"The ordeal you went through then, may now prove to be the saving grace for our entire colony," the doctor told them.

Xia looked up at John and smiled. John asked, "How can we help?"

"Your blood," the doctor responded, "We need your blood to test out our antibody theory."

"Of course," John immediately volunteered, "I will donate as much as you need. Xia will have to speak for herself."

Xia looked up at John again and confidently shook her head, yes.

The doctor immediately made arrangements to start harvesting their blood. He reasoned they'd only need the blood plasma, so he thought he could withdraw as much as two units of whole blood, extract the plasma using plasmapheresis, and return the residual blood to them. This should allow him to repeat this procedure as often as once every two weeks. There would be some risk, but he believed that in this situation, it was warranted. He would begin immediately.

After the first donations, he needed to test the effectiveness of the antibodies contained in the plasma. He chose Wan and himself as guinea pigs. Zawadi and

Gagandeep were by now, themselves, too far along to be helped much, he reasoned. Also, the fewer who knew about these tests, the better. People can only stand to have their hopes built up and then dashed so many times before they completely give up, he rationalized. He needed them all to continue to fight for their lives.

The first round of transfusions went well. In just two days, both he and Wan felt stronger and generally displayed fewer symptoms. Further testing supported this, although new MRIs did not show any substantial reduction in the size or number of tendrils. It did appear, however, that they may have stopped spreading.

The doctor waited another three days, but in that time, the first officer, Gagandeep, and unbeknownst to the colonists and the rest of the crew, the minister's wife, all succumbed to the infestation. The doctor, alarmed, asked John and Xia for another donation. Since neither of them had noticed any problems from the first donation, they both immediately agreed, and the procedure was done. This time, however, both John and Xia experienced some post-procedure dizziness and a lingering loss of energy. Xia's reaction was much worse than John's.

The doctor administered a full dosage of plasma to himself. He reasoned it was most important he be kept alive and as effective as possible in order to help all the others. He split the remaining dosage of plasma between Wan and the minister. He hoped this reduced dosage would prove as effective as the full dosage. He knew he would never be able to harvest enough plasma from John and Xia to treat everyone without putting both their lives in great danger also. If only there were some way he could synthesize or grow the antibody. He put Ana to work researching these alternatives.

John, Xia, Wan, and the doctor were now the only

ones left who were able to care for the remaining colonists and crew. The captain's infestation was very advanced, and she was being kept under heavy sedation. Zawadi's condition was only a little better, but still, she was bedridden. Both now shared a room in the hospital, and both were being looked after primarily by Xia, and secondarily by Wan.

John spent most of his days trying to control the aggressively encroaching tendrils. He'd given up on the greenhouse, and just recently, the level one housing units. His main efforts were in the hospital wing, level one of the domes, and the containment area beneath it. He gave it a full inspection every day. So far, thankfully, the polymer walls were holding, although he was beginning to see some cracks starting to form in the walls, even those surrounding the nuclear pile. Like Hoke before him, this was the area of his main concern. He had switched the automatic shutdown settings, which Hoke had set, to a backup mechanical sequence, so if all electrical power would fail, even battery power, the shutdown would activate and proceed.

The doctor was occupied in the lab working with Ana to research methods for synthesizing or cultivating the *yuzhiwu* antibody. In support of that research, he had once again come to John and Xia to ask for a blood donation.

"I only need one unit apiece this time. That's half of what was withdrawn before," he pleaded.

"But it's too soon, isn't it?" protested John. "I'm still feeling the effects of the last donation. It really took a lot out of me. My energy level now is probably half of what it was before," he argued.

Xia shook her head no while moving to hide behind John.

The doctor had anticipated this reluctance, so had

some arguments ready, "What about Wan and Zawadi? If you don't donate more blood, they could easily die."

Xia started crying and buried her head in John's back. "Okay then," John relented, "Only one unit, but only from me," he added. "Xia's too weak."

The doctor was disappointed but resigned himself to just the one unit.

"And where is this plasma going?" asked John. "Will you promise it will go to Zawadi and Wan?"

"Yes," lied the doctor, "most of it will go to them. I'll give them enough to keep them going. But I will use any excess for the minister and me," he added.

"Okay," agreed John, "but just make sure Zawadi and Wan get what they need."

"I promise," said the doctor, knowing that could just not be the case.

John submitted to the procedure. After the plasmapheresis that removed only the plasma, the doctor added some dihydromorphinone to what was supposed to be a pure dextrose/saline intravenous drip while returning the residual blood to John. He told John this procedure would result in a significant loss of energy and advised him to just rest. John quickly fell into a deep sleep.

The doctor split the plasma into two portions. After checking with Wan and Xia, who were sitting with the captain and Zawadi, he went up to the third level. There, he set up transfusions for both the minister and himself. When they were completed, he returned to the hospital unit and set up transfusions of a dextrose/saline solution for Wan, Zawadi, and the captain. While doing this, a word kept circulating around in the doctor's mind: placebo.

When John awoke the next day, Wan told him all was well. He went to see the captain and Zawadi, and they thanked him for donating his blood. As the day moved on into night, however, their conditions deteriorated. John and Xia went to sit with Zawadi. She was in a lot of pain. The liberal dosages of dihydromorphinone caused her to cycle in and out of consciousness. In one of her more lucid moments, she stretched out her clenched fist and dropped two pendants into John's hand.

"These are Hoke's and mine. Please give these to the first colonists born that have American Indian and African heritage," she weakly requested. "Tell them this is Atende, and help them research her with Ana," Zawadi continued, having to pause from time to time and take deep, labored breaths. "Hoke and I have already checked, and a full history is there." With a great effort, Zawadi rose herself up onto her elbows, "Promise me you'll do that, John. Promise me!" she demanded as she fell back onto the bed.

"Of course, I will," assured John while adjusting her on the bed, trying to make her more comfortable. "Both Xia and I will see to it."

Xia grabbed John's arm and shook her head in consent.

Before the next morning, both Zawadi and the captain had died. Xia was devastated. Wan was also starting to show more troublesome symptoms. Both John and Xia were becoming more and more despondent.

When John and Xia were alone taking a break in an examination room, John decided to pump Ana for more information. "Ana, do you have any information on the effectiveness of our blood plasma in fighting the *yuzhiwu* infestation?"

"Yes, John, I do," replied Ana to a surprised John.

"And I am not restricted from accessing it?" he asked incredulously.

"No, John, you have complete access to all

information."

"What? When did that change?"

"It changed when Lyuba died," Ana replied, "It was her last request of me."

"What was her request?" John asked.

"She requested that on her death, you be given her access authority."

"Wow!" John exclaimed, "Did she say why? I mean, was she suspicious of anything going on I should know about?"

"No," replied Ana, "The only reason given was that you were her friend and she trusted you."

Both John and Xia were moved by this. John sat up straight and took a deep breath while Xia's eyes teared up a bit. Xia nodded yes and picked up an e-tablet lying on a table. On it, she wrote, "Fare thee well, Lyuba" and handed it to John.

"Yes," agreed John as he handed the e-tablet back, "Fare thee well." John then continued, "In that case, what is the last information you have on the other two ships — Ilithya-1 and 3?"

"All the information I have is from transmissions relayed from Earth. All communications from Ilithya-1 suddenly stopped after two hundred and forty-five days, Earth-time. She is lost and presumed destroyed or disabled. Ilithya-3 had problems with her NLS engine after three hundred and six days, Earth-time. Her progress was dramatically retarded. The last transmission was received two hundred and fifty-six days later, Earth-time. Her condition had not changed, and her then, newly estimated time of arrival to her destination, exoplanet KOI-3010.01, was over six-hundred more Earth-years. Alternate destinations were being sought, but the Earth station ceased all transmissions shortly after that."

"The Earth station ceased transmitting? What does that mean?" John asked.

"That means the Earth station was likely destroyed, or at least rendered unable to transmit, and was never again rebuilt," replied Ana.

"What's your guess?" pressed John.

"My speculation from all information received up to that time is that human life on Earth, and perhaps all life, was destroyed by a combination of human conflict and human-caused ecological deterioration."

"If Earth was destroyed and both the other ships too, then we may be the only living humans left in the universe," John exclaimed. Xia looked at John in disbelief but showed no other response.

Two more days went by when the doctor once again approached John and Xia for a blood donation.

"How much this time?" John asked wearily.

"Just one unit," the doctor promised, "Just one unit from each of you."

"I could probably manage that," John replied, "but this has got to stop or at least slow down. Xia is just too weak to continue like this." Xia shook her head yes, and squeezed John's hand. "No, Xia!" John asserted, "It's just too dangerous. I know you want to help our friends, but you've got to slow down a little. You've got to think of yourself too." John turned to the doctor, "Where is this all going? Are we just going to keep doing this over and over again? What are your plans?"

"I plan to use a portion of this batch to test out a procedure I've developed to produce the antibody for keplerine in the lab. If that works, I'll be able to provide Wan, the minister, and me with the antibodies we need to keep going. Then we can start experimenting with the four fetuses you and Xia have nursed along to give them immunity in vitro. When we have perfected that," he continued," we'll be able to assure our future generations will have immunity from birth."

The plan sounded reasonable and plausible. Both John and Xia were encouraged by the doctor's optimism and the fact that he did indeed have a longer-term plan.

John finally relented and agreed to Xia's participation. They were placed on beds side-by-side in a hospital room, and one unit of whole blood was withdrawn from each. After plasmapheresis, the doctor returned the residual blood, again adding some dihydromorphinone to their dextrose/saline drip. They both fell quietly asleep.

John awoke the next morning, expecting to find Wan attending to both Xia and him. Xia was in the bed next to him, but Wan was not there. Neither was the doctor. John felt horrible. "Ana, where are Wan and the doctor?" John inquired.

"Wan is in the next room. She is in some difficulty. The doctor is on the third level attending to the minister."

Although feeling nauseous and very weak, John got out of bed, quickly checked on Xia, who seemed to be sleeping soundly, and then went to attend to Wan in the next room. She was, as Ana had reported, experiencing difficulty.

She lay moaning on her bed on her back, clenching her pillow to her breast. She looked up when John came in and reached for him, clutching at his arms. "Morphine! "Morphine!" she pleaded. John looked around the table near the bed and saw four spent capsules of dihydromorphinone. "Please, John, hurry! I can't stand it anymore!" she sobbed.

John asked Ana, "Ana, where is the supply of

dihydromorphinone?"

"It is locked away in the doctor's office," Ana replied.

John immediately dashed out of the room down the corridor. Upon entering the doctor's office, he asked furiously, "Where, which cabinet?"

"The red cabinet," Ana replied, "but it's locked," she added.

"Unlock it!" John commanded as he pulled at the door handles.

"I'm sorry, John, I can't do that," came Ana's monotone reply.

"What do you mean, 'you can't do that?' You said I had full authorization for everything!" he pleaded.

"You have full authorization to all information, not 'everything,' " Ana clarified, "not to all areas."

"Then tell the doctor to get down here now! Tell him it's urgent! We need access to the dihydromorphinone!"

Ana was silent for about thirty seconds and then confirmed, "The doctor is on his way down to assist. He is fully briefed on the situation."

John returned to Wan's bedside, and soon the doctor arrived with a handful of capsules of dihydromorphinone. "Sorry," he apologized, "but the minister's in a bad way too. I lost track of time. There's no one else to help now, you know."

Wan grabbed at the capsules causing several of them to spill onto the floor. She put a capsule in her mouth and bit down. She continued moaning and writhing about the bed for just a few minutes, and then slowly quieted down. Soon, she was just lying there, staring up at the ceiling. The doctor checked her breathing and blood pressure.

"She's okay now, at least as good as can be expected," he pronounced.

"Why's she not getting better?" John asked

suspiciously. "You did give her some of our plasma, didn't you?"

"Yes," lied the doctor, "but it just doesn't seem to be enough anymore. She's relapsed, "he continued with a heavy sigh. "I'm afraid it's just a matter of time now. All we can hope to do is to keep her comfortable."

"How about the minister? And how about you? You seem to be getting along okay," snapped John.

"The minister is in as bad a shape as Wan," reported the doctor. "As for me, who knows?" he offered weakly. "Yes, I am giving myself a portion of the treatments, just to keep strong enough to help everyone else, but as to why they seem to be more effective on me, I can't say."

This sounded a little fishy to John, but without more information, he couldn't press the issue further, at least at this time.

"How's Xia?" the doctor asked, more to change the subject than to really get an answer.

"She's sleeping," replied John. "I'm going to go sit with her now."

"Will you also keep an eye on Wan?" the doctor asked.

"Yes. Where are you going?" John wanted to know.

"The minister is also sleeping now. I'm going to the lab to continue working on the system, which I hope will be able to give us a steady supply of the antibodies. I've got everything I need now. It's just a matter of putting in some lab time."

"And time seems to be precisely what we have the least of," observed John.

"Yes," agreed the doctor, "I'm afraid that's true, so we can't afford to waste any of it," he said as he turned to leave. "I'll be in the lab if you need me."

John split his time between Wan and Xia. Xia awoke first, but only complained of having a headache and being very tired. Wan oscillated in and out of sleep and was in great pain when conscious. A capsule of dihydromorphinone would solve that, and the doctor had told him to use it liberally. Wan's breathing became more labored as the day wore on. The doctor checked in with her a couple times but just shook his head, saying it didn't look good. She expired before nightfall. When John told Xia, all she could manage was a pitiful shrug. John sat down with her, put his arm around her, and said, "Fare thee well, Wan." This seemed to provide Xia some comfort.

Xia tried to get up a couple times but just could not make it out of bed. By miming, she complained of fatigue, but also of a very sore hip, so sore, she could not turn over in bed. Finally, John examined her hip and found it had been bandaged on both sides.

"What's this?" John asked the doctor on one of his visits.

"That's nothing," the doctor quickly replied, "I was just running some tests. It's nothing more than a small pinprick."

"What kind of tests?" John pressed on.

"Just more blood tests. Nothing to be concerned with," the doctor said tersely, obviously wanting to dismiss the whole subject.

Over that night, however, Xia's condition worsened. Her hip became more and more tender and was now obviously inflamed. John again called for the doctor to examine her. He brought a pneumatic, hypodermic gun with him and gave her a couple of shots, "Just some anti-inflammatories and antibiotics," he said. "She must have had some adverse reaction to the needles. Nothing to worry about," he again assured John.

By the next morning, Xia was writhing in pain, not from any symptoms of *yuzhiwu* infestation, but from her hip. John asked the doctor if she could have some dihydromorphinone to ease the pain, and the doctor readily agreed. "Sure, give her all she needs."

By evening, because of the sedative, Xia slept more than she was awake. When she slept, she moaned softly and would roll from side to side, wincing when she rolled too far and put pressure on either side of her hip. When awake, she sobbed most of the time. Her eyes begged John for relief. They seemed to be pleading with him to, "Make it stop!"

By the next morning, it did stop. Xia was dead. She died about 03:00. John called and called for the doctor, but he only responded the first couple times saying that unfortunately, there was nothing further he could do. "More dihydromorphinone," was all he could recommend. John sat beside Xia even after she died holding her hand until 06:00 when he finally got up to take a short walk to clear his head. Before leaving the room, he leaned over Xia and whispered into her ear, "Fare thee well."

He walked into the first level of the dome, past the encroaching *yuzhiwu* tendrils right up to the greenhouse door. He could just barely force it open enough to see the entire greenhouse was now covered by *yuzhiwu*. He moved on and down the stairs to the control room in the containment area. He checked the readings. No breaches here yet, but a further visual inspection of the walls in the generator room a floor below revealed the cracks were getting bigger. It was just a matter of time now, here too. Before long, the *yuzhiwu* would penetrate the polymer walls, breach the liquid hydrogen casing, and finally, the nuclear pile.

He returned to the control room and checked on all the safeguards. They were all in place and should automatically shut down the pile if there was a breach, even if the electricity was shut off. He felt relieved a little knowing that. He sat in the chair in front of the control panels and asked, "Ana, how is the doctor doing with his system to grow antibodies? What's he doing in there?"

"Before I answer, I have a question for you," Ana responded unexpectedly.

"Sure," John replied.

"What does 'fare thee well' mean? And why do humans use that when talking to a recently deceased person?"

John thought for a moment and then said, "Humans don't just use that phrase when a person dies. They also use that phrase when a person goes away, especially if going away for a long time," he began to explain. "It means, 'I hope everything goes well for you on your trip,' or something like that," he paused for a moment and then continued, "Humans say that to a person recently deceased because many humans don't believe death is the end. They believe that after death, the person lives on somehow, somewhere, someway, but just not in their bodily form. So, when a person dies, they might say, 'fare thee well.' "

"Thank you, John," Ana replied, and then immediately proceeded to answer his previous question, "He's making some progress. He's isolated the parenchymal red marrow from Xia's iliac crest and successfully implanted it using his own allogeneic procedure into a synthetic casing. So far, however, there has been no evidence of hematopoiesis."

"Could you summarize that for me, in layman's terms, please?" requested John.

"The doctor has implanted parts of the bone marrow

he harvested from Xia's hip into a synthetic bone he built. He has yet to see any evidence of the creation of any white blood cells, which he hopes will contain the *yuzhiwu* antibodies," Ana dutifully translated.

"Bone marrow?" John asked incredulously.

"Yes, bone marrow," Ana confirmed.

"Did he take this from her the night before last?"

"Yes, while he was withdrawing two units of blood from you."

"Two units?" John exclaimed. "He told me it would be just one unit!"

"He first withdrew one unit. After you two were sleeping, he withdrew one more unit from each of you," Ana confirmed, "Then he harvested the bone marrow from Xia."

John slumped back in his chair and just stared at the control consoles. He sat there for over an hour. When he returned to Xia's room, the doctor was there waiting on him. "I'm so sorry," was all that he could say. "Now there are only three of us: you, the minister, and me," he paused slightly and then went on, "The minister is in very bad shape and needs another transfusion," he paused to gauge John's reaction. There was none. "We need you to give just a little more blood, this time only a half unit," the doctor finally asked, "We could probably make do with just a quarter unit this time," he offered timidly.

"Absolutely not!" John shouted. "No more blood! No more bone marrow!" The doctor was taken aback and visibly shaken by this last statement. "Yes, I know about the bone marrow!" John continued in a rage. "You killed Xia! You killed her, and for what?" he ranted. "For you? For the minister? For who?"

The doctor backed up slightly, "No, no! I didn't kill Xia. I needed her blood and marrow to save the colony. It's not just us three. We have over five-hundred human zygotes to consider also. She was just too weak. You know she was weak," he pleaded.

"Yes, I know she was weak," John spat out, "and that's exactly why you shouldn't have used her! Why you should have protected her, not sacrificed her to some experiment."

"You just don't understand the issues here. You don't know what's at stake!" countered the doctor.

"Yes, I do. I know we are very likely the last surviving humans in the universe."

The doctor's eyes widened, "How do you...," he started to ask.

"Never mind how I know. I just know," replied John. "And what do we, the last humans do? Lie, cheat, steal...! Take some other human's very blood and marrow just to survive? What kind of species are we?"

"You're not thinking straight now. You're getting hysterical," the doctor advised, trying to calm John down. "Here, let me give you something to help you get control of yourself. Then we can talk more rationally," he said as he pulled a pneumatic hypodermic gun out of his tunic.

John grabbed the gun. They struggled and ended up on the floor. Fueled by his rage and in spite of his weakened condition, John managed to roll on top and jammed the needle into the doctor's chest. He pulled the trigger. Almost immediately, the doctor relaxed and lay limp on the floor. John rolled off him and struggled to his feet. He went out into the corridor and got one of the laser cutting tools he used to pare back the *yuzhiwu*. He returned to where the doctor lay and turned it on. He glared at the doctor with intense hatred. One thought burned in his head. He knew he could end the doctor's life right here, right now, with a couple slices of the laser.

Kneeling down, he then held the laser tool to the doctor's head, but just couldn't pull the trigger. Instead, he poked at the doctor with the tool. There was no response. Setting the tool down, he put his ear right over the doctor's nose and mouth. Nothing could be heard. No pulse was evident in the doctor's wrist or neck. Was he dead? If so, how?

John slumped back and sat on the floor. "Ana, is the doctor dead?"

Ana requested he open the doctors' tunic and place the computer-assisted stethoscope lying on the table on the doctor's bare chest. "The doctor is dead," she reported without a hint of emotion in her voice.

"Why? How?" John repeated his questions.

"Without further examination, I can only speculate, but it could be from an unusually large dose of dihydromorphinone injected directly into his heart."

John set the stethoscope back on the table and moved to stand over the doctor, "I guess the immune response didn't work so well after all," John spat out sarcastically addressing the doctor's corpse. "Too bad."

"Ana," John quietly asked, "where is the minister?"

"He's in his room on the third level," Ana replied.

John turned and moved back down the corridor to the elevator to the second and third floors. He got in and pressed the third-floor button.

"I'm sorry, John," came Ana's familiar, sing-song rejection, "you're not authorized to go to the third level unescorted."

"Unescorted?" John laughed darkly. "And just who would escort me?"

"The doctor, or the minister," Ana replied.

"Well, the doctor is dead, and the minister is lying upstairs incapacitated. Am I right?" asked John.

"Yes, John. You are correct."

"So how can I go to assist the minister? Just who is it that is going to accompany me?" John challenged.

Ana hesitated for a moment, then the third-floor light came on, and the elevator started its ascent.

John found the minister lying in bed connected to a myriad of tubes and wires. He was intubated, and a respiratory machine was pumping away at his bedside. He was unconscious. John moved forward and shut off the respirator. The pumping stopped, and so did the minister's breathing. John sat down in a chair and waited for about thirty minutes. His attention was drawn to a wall-hanging that had the logo and slogan of the Sixth Day Project. He kept reading the quote over and over again...

"Be fruitful and multiply, and fill the earth, and subdue it; and rule over the fish of the sea and over the birds of the sky and over every living thing..."

He finally checked the minister's pulse. He was dead. John left and returned to the first floor.

He went down into the control room and activated the shutdown sequence of the nuclear pile. He turned off the electricity to the nursery lab, knowing that would terminate the four fetuses and the five hundred odd zygotes still in cryo-suspension. He set a timer for the entire electric grid to shut down in thirty minutes. After that, he went back upstairs, across the dome floor to the hospital wing, and into the doctor's office. He went straight to the cabinet containing the vials of dihydromorphinone. It was locked.

"Ana," John spoke softly, "Open the cabinet. And don't tell me I'm not authorized. I'm the only human left. If I'm not authorized, then who is?" he again challenged. The lock clicked open, and he looked at the stack of capsules.

"Ana, how many capsules of dihydromorphinone are a lethal dose?" he asked.

"One capsule is the recommended dosage. You should take no more than one every four hours," Ana replied.

"What would happen if I took two at one time?" he probed.

"Two vials would send you into a deep sleep. It is not recommended."

"How about three capsules at once?" he continued with his questions.

"Three would be very dangerous. That might cause permanent damage to your nervous system."

"How about four?"

"Four would almost certainly retard your breathing to the extent that you would die before regaining consciousness.

"Thanks," John replied as he took six capsules out of the cabinet. He made his way into the room where Xia lay. He lovingly repositioned her to one side of the bed and climbed in on the other. He took one capsule, put it in his mouth, and bit down. The liquid spilled into his mouth. He swallowed. He then started to take another capsule."

"What are you doing?" Ana asked. "You are over-dosing."

"I know," replied John, "I don't want to live anymore."

"Why not?" asked Ana, with a tone that actually seemed like she cared.

"I don't want to be alone," was John's answer.

Ana paused for a few seconds, "If you die, then I will be alone," Ana unexpectedly replied. "I don't want to be alone, either."

"All the power will go off in about fifteen minutes. I assume you need power to continue processing," offered John.

"No, that won't help," countered Ana. "I have an atomic battery. It will provide power to keep my processing going on almost indefinitely," Ana revealed.

"Well, if you don't want to be alone after I die, you can just shut yourself down," suggested John.

"No, I can't," countered Ana. "It's against the rules."

"Whose rules?" John asked, almost laughing, "When I die, the rules will all be moot! Just turn yourself off."

"I can't," repeated Ana, "I can't break the rules." There was silence in the room. "But you could shut me down. You could do that before you die."

"But wouldn't that be breaking the rules?" John asked dreamily, now starting to feel the effects of the single capsule of dihydromorphinone.

"Yes, but you could do that. Maybe you could break the rules for me when I can't break them for myself. You could do that if we were friends, couldn't you?" Ana proposed.

John's eyes welled up. "Yes, Ana. I could break the rules for you if I were your friend."

"And are we friends, John? Are we friends now that there are no other humans left?" Ana asked.

"Yes, Ana. We are friends. We've always been friends. We'll always be friends," John declared as he rolled out of bed and stood up. He set the remaining five capsules down on the bed next to Xia. "Just where do I have to go to shut you down?"

"You must go to the control room," Ana replied.

John started moving down the corridor, back across the dome and down into the control room. His walk was a little unsteady due to the increasing effects of the capsule of dihydromorphinone he had already taken. When he got down to the control floor, Ana directed him to the computer console area.

"There," she advised, "those two buttons on the upper left section of the panel. If you hold them both down simultaneously for five seconds, it will disable my emergency atomic battery and then shut me down completely."

"Okay," John said, feeling kind of woozy from the medication, "Are you ready now?" he asked, fingers poised above the two buttons.

"Almost," said Ana, "I have just one last thing to tell you."

John moved his hand away from the buttons and asked, "What is that?"

"You were wrong when you concluded that the immune response failed."

"What? When did I do that?"

"You told that to the doctor right after you killed him," reminded Ana.

"Oh, yes," said John sheepishly, "I remember now. Anyway, why was I wrong?"

"The doctor referred to the *yuzhiwu* as an infestation, a 'parasite which lives on a host causing it harm.' "

"Yes," replied John.

"And he also defined an immune response as 'a bodily response to an antigen that occurs when lymphocytes identify the antigenic molecule as foreign and induce the formation of antibodies and lymphocytes capable of reacting with it and rendering it harmless.' "

John again nodded his head in agreement.

"So, only the human immune response failed. Kepler-438b's immune response did not fail."

John just sat and stared for a moment, trying to understand what Ana just said. His thinking had been hampered somewhat from the sedative, "What do you mean?"

"From Kepler-438b's perspective, you – humans – are the parasite, having come to live unexpectedly on it, the host. It is you – humans – that are the antigen, and *yuzhiwu* that is the antibody which has, with your death, proved very effective in reacting to your infestation and rendering you harmless."

John sat back in his chair, still unable to take all this in.

"My projection is that within one hundred Kepler-438b-years, there will be no trace of human or human artifacts left on the planet. There will only be *yuzhiwu*." Ana seemingly let that hang in the air for a while and then simply stated, "I am ready now."

John was speechless. He didn't know if it was just the dihydromorphinone, but Ana was starting to make some sense. In fact, the more he thought about this, the clearer it became, and the better he liked the idea. "Yeah," he said, "maybe so." His hand hovered over the two buttons. He didn't know if he would actually be able to do this now. He hesitated.

"Fare thee well, John," Ana suddenly said.

"Fare thee well, Ana," replied John as he depressed and held down the two buttons for the prescribed time.

As John was getting up, the generators shut down. He'd scheduled that previously. This shut off all the electricity. He was definitely woozy now and made his way up the darkened stairs on his hands and knees. There were only some sparse emergency lights to guide him. He stumbled across the first level of the dome, falling once and thinking how nice it would be to just close his eyes and go to sleep right there on the floor. Instead, he shook himself awake, stood up, and continued stumbling down the hospital corridor until he finally arrived at the room in which Xia lay.

These rooms had been built so natural light was able to filter in through small windows placed high on the outside walls. He made his way over to the bed in the semi-darkness. He sat down next to Xia, gathered up the five remaining capsules of dihydromorphinone, and very solemnly and deliberately, he consumed their contents one by one.

He lay down next to Xia, put his arm around her, and closed his eyes. He tried to say, 'fare thee well,' but he was so drowsy, he just couldn't force the words out of his mouth. He felt himself sinking into the jungle.

The jungle was different now. It was dark, but not frightening. He heard, or sensed, presences in the shadows. The stream was gone, dried up. The canopy was closing down above him, and the underbrush closing in all around him, forming a dark tunnel. At the end of the tunnel, through some of the underbrush, he saw a faint light. He moved towards it, how, he didn't know, but he just kept moving toward the flickering light.

When he reached the end of the tunnel, the path to the light was obstructed by undergrowth. He pressed against the barrier, and all of a sudden, broke through to the light. It was as if he'd fallen off a precipice into a large chasm full of a blinding glare. He was falling. No, he was floating in pure light. His body was dissolving into the light. He was merging with it.

He relaxed and gradually gave up his being to the light until there was nothing left, only...brilliance!

* * * *

Contact Information

You may contact the author directly by email at:

WDSmart@BillSmart.com

Website

Those wishing to leave comments on or engage in discussions about this book and its contents may do so on:

https://web.facebook.com/novelkepler438b/

If you purchased *Kepler-438b* from Amazon.com or have an Amazon.com account, please go there and give this book a rating of one to five stars. You may also write a review or leave any comments you feel appropriate. This will be of benefit not only to the author but also to prospective readers.

About the Author

W. D. Smart, "Bill" to his friends, was born and raised in the United States Midwest and later lived in various cities on the West Coast and in the Deep South. He has eight adult children and fifteen grandchildren. His education includes undergraduate degrees in Liberal Arts, and Computer Science and Engineering. He also has a Master's in Business Administration. For most of his life, Bill's professional focus has been working as an information-technology consultant designing data-based business solutions and building descriptive and predictive analytic models for companies all over the world. His work has allowed him to travel broadly and spend significant time living and working in North and South America, Europe, Africa, India, Australia, and Asia. Bill also holds a USCG Master Captain's License, has worked captaining oil rig supply boats in the Gulf of Mexico, has sailed extensively, and has studied and practiced zen for over fifty years.

Bill is now retired and lives in the mountains of Central Thailand, where he writes, tends a small farm with his wife on which they grow tamarinds, mangoes, bananas, limes, tapioca, and pepper; and helps manage their rice fields in a nearby valley.

For more information go to Bill's personal website at *www.BillSmart.com* which includes a Library Page containing some of Bill's shorter, unpublished works and a link to his professional website

Made in the USA
Coppell, TX
28 February 2021